Praise for

Halfway Normal

★ "Readers will feel with her as Norah struggles with how, when, and to whom she should tell her story—if at all. The moment that really sings is when Norah realizes that there are some life experiences that change you forever, and that's not always a bad thing. Dee, whose acknowledgments hint at family experience with childhood cancer, does an exceptional job accurately depicting Norah's struggles in a way that is translatable to those with varied understanding of illness. . . . A powerful story not only about illness, but about accepting yourself for who you are—no matter the experiences that shaped you."
—*Kirkus Reviews,* starred review

★ "A powerful story about surviving and thriving after serious illness." —*School Library Journal,* starred review

"The authenticity of Norah's story can be credited to the author's own experiences as the mother of a cancer patient. But this is not a book about cancer; rather, it's about the process of moving forward in its wake. Readers who appreciate well-wrought portrayals of transformative middle-school experiences, such as Rebecca Stead's *Goodbye Stranger* (2015), will find a story in a similar spirit here." —*Booklist*

"In writing this remarkable novel, Barbara Dee has performed an amazing feat. She has traveled to places you hope you will never have to go and then drawn a lovely, heartbreaking, warm, funny, and ultimately hopeful map of the way back home."
—**Jordan Sonnenblick,** author of
DRUMS, GIRLS, AND DANGEROUS PIE

"Barbara Dee has an unfailing sense of the dynamics of middle school social life. Spot-on portrayals of friends and family relationships frame a powerful main character who's determined to find her way back. *Halfway Normal* has a brave, kind heart—as tender and triumphant as the main character herself."
—**Karen Romano Young,** author of
HUNDRED PERCENT

"Dee realistically explores the varied emotions of maturing middle-school students, as well as the way Norah feels singled out and patronized by classmates and adults alike."
—*Publishers Weekly*

Praise for

Star-Crossed

"A sweet story of young love amid middle school theatrics . . . Readers cannot but help root for Mattie as she discovers bravery she never gave herself credit for, both onstage and in life." —*Kirkus Reviews*

"A sweet coming-out story for junior high readers. The clever Shakespeare content is a bonus. . . . Verdict: A fine choice for middle school libraries in need of accessible LGBTQ stories, and a great option for students reading or performing *Romeo and Juliet*." —*School Library Journal*

"In this welcome addition to the middle grade LGBTQ bookshelf . . . Dee (*Truth or Dare*) thoughtfully dramatizes the intricate social performance of middle school, with its secret crushes and fierce rivalries." —*Publishers Weekly*

ALSO BY BARBARA DEE

HALFWAY NORMAL

BARBARA DEE

Aladdin

NEW YORK LONDON TORONTO SYDNEY NEW DELHI

For Alex

ALADDIN

An imprint of Simon & Schuster Children's Publishing Division
1230 Avenue of the Americas, New York, New York 10020
First Aladdin paperback edition September 2018
Text copyright © 2017 by Barbara Dee
Cover illustration and hand-lettering copyright © 2017 by Jenna Stempel
Also available in an Aladdin hardcover edition.
All rights reserved, including the right of reproduction in whole or in part in any form.
ALADDIN and related logo are registered trademarks of Simon & Schuster, Inc.
For information about special discounts for bulk purchases, please contact
Simon & Schuster Special Sales at 1-866-506-1949 or business@simonandschuster.com.
The Simon & Schuster Speakers Bureau can bring authors to your live event.
For more information or to book an event contact the Simon & Schuster Speakers Bureau
at 1-866-248-3049 or visit our website at www.simonspeakers.com.
Art direction by Jessica Handelman
Interior designed by Greg Stadnyk
The text of this book was set in Neutraface.
Manufactured in the United States of America 0319 OFF
4 6 8 10 9 7 5 3
The Library of Congress has cataloged the hardcover edition as follows:
Names: Dee, Barbara, author.
Title: Halfway normal / by Barbara Dee.
Description: First Aladdin hardcover edition. | New York : Aladdin, 2017. |
Summary: Twelve-year-old cancer survivor Norah struggles to fit in
at middle school after two years of treatment, but she finds her voice with
the help of new friend Griffin, who shares her love of mythology.
Identifiers: LCCN 2017003893 (print) | LCCN 2017031288 (eBook) |
ISBN 9781481478533 (eBook) | ISBN 9781481478519 (hardcover)
Subjects: | CYAC: Middle schools—Fiction. |
Schools—Fiction. | Friendship—Fiction. |
Leukemia—Fiction. | Family problems—Fiction. |
BISAC: JUVENILE FICTION / Social Issues / New Experience. |
JUVENILE FICTION / Social Issues / Friendship. |
JUVENILE FICTION / Social Issues / Emotions & Feelings. |
Classification: LCC PZ7.D35867 (eBook) | LCC PZ7.D35867 Hal 2017 (print) |
DDC [Fic]—dc23
LC record available at https://lccn.loc.gov/2017003893
ISBN 9781481478526 (pbk)

THE GIRL WHO

The second I stepped into the room, somebody screamed. I turned to look behind me—for a rock star, or a grizzly bear, or the Loch Ness Monster. But no one was following. The scream was for me.

"Norah Levy! Omigod! *It's Norah Levy!*" Two girls jumped up from their chairs to smother me in a hug. Kylie Shen and Aria Maldonado, who smelled like bubblegum-scented shampoo. Or shampoo-scented bubblegum.

"Hey, hi," I managed to say.

They pulled away.

"Omigod, *Norah*, this is so great, how *are* you?" Kylie squealed. She had the kind of voice that took over a room, even though she was tiny. Not as tiny as me, though.

"Pretty good, actually," I said.

"Well, you *look* amazing," Aria said. She gave me a pep-talk sort of smile and bounced on her toes.

"Incredible," Kylie agreed. "And I love your hair!"

"Yeah, Norah, you look so cute in a pixie cut."

I ruffled my hair, much shorter than it used to be, but finally long enough to be a style. "Thanks. It dries really fast. And no tangles, so."

"I wish my mom would let me get a short haircut," Aria said. Which was insane. Besides, with her warm brown skin and her height, no way could Aria look like me, even if she got permission.

"Everyone, please take your seats," boomed the homeroom teacher, a man I didn't know from before. A gym teacher, by the look of his track pants.

Kylie grabbed my arm. "You're sitting with us, Norah," she informed me.

"Hey, aren't you the girl who—" Now a boy I didn't recognize was talking to me. Oh, wait a sec. Right. His name was Malik. Malik Thrash. As if it was possible to forget a name like that.

"Malik, don't be rude," Aria snapped at him.

"I'm not rude," he protested. "How was I being rude?"

"You shouldn't make Norah talk about it."

"It's okay," I said. "Yes, I'm definitely The Girl Who."

"That's so funny. *The Girl Who*. I like that!" Kylie laughed, a little too enthusiastically.

Malik looked confused. "Sorry, Norah. I just didn't expect to see you. I heard—"

Aria and Kylie popped their eyes at him.

"People should shut their mouths if they don't know what they're talking about," Kylie said. "And they should *also* consider other people's feelings." She petted my arm. "Don't pay *any* attention to him, Norah."

"It's fine," I said.

I realized then that everyone was watching us. Delete that: They were watching *me*. Mostly, they were giving me out-of-the-corner-of-their-eyes looks, like they were trying to be subtle, but a few kids were flat-out staring. So I wiggled my fingers in a sort of general hi, but they got embarrassed and turned away.

What was that about? Were they doing a before-and-after? Maybe I looked weirder than I thought I did. I patted my hair with a sweaty hand and tugged at my orange tee. Why hadn't I protested when Mom bought me *orange*? And why had I put it on this morning? I looked like a Cheeto in a hazmat suit.

Then I pretended to read my schedule. First period was math, where at least I'd be with my best friend, Harper. (I knew this because I'd texted her the second my schedule showed up in my mailbox; she called back to tell me gossip about all the teachers, including how our math teacher handed out Smarties during tests.) My other good friend, Silas, wasn't in math with us, but maybe we'd be together in English or science. So if I could just make it through morning homeroom—

"Norah Levy?" the homeroom teacher called as he hung up the classroom phone. "You're wanted in Guidance."

"Now?" I glanced at the clock. "But it's almost first period."

"Right. Ms. Castro says she needs to see you *before* first."

"You want me to come with you, Norah?" Aria asked.

I looked at her. "What for?"

"Just . . . you know, so you don't get lost."

"I can find it. But thanks." I stuffed my schedule into my backpack. In some zippered pocket was a map of the building, but I'd check it in the hallway. Not here.

"Whoa, your backpack looks heavy," Malik said. "If you want, Norah, I could help—"

"Nope, thanks, got it," I said.

A girl moved her chair out of the way to let me pass. "Sorry," she murmured. Apologizing for what? The fact that her chair had been in my way, and now wasn't? The fact that everyone was acting like I was made of cloud wisps and dandelion fluff, and one false move and I'd blow away forever?

"No problem," I said, feeling the scorch of everyone's eyes as I fled the room.

ALL BEHIND YOU NOW

Some nights in the hospital when I couldn't sleep, I played a game called Room. The way you played was: You picked a real room from real life and tried to name as many details as possible. This was so boring it usually put you to sleep right away, which of course was the whole point of the game.

Although once in a while it didn't work—and you ended up wasting hours and hours just lying there, thinking about the room you'd picked, listing all the chairs and ceiling cracks and books on the bookshelves. And then, if you ever did return to that room, you still had a weird feeling about it in your stomach. Like: *Why did you keep me up all night, Room? What did I ever do to you, anyway?*

The funny thing was, this was exactly how I felt as I sat in Ms. Castro's office. She was the seventh grade guidance counselor, so obviously I couldn't have been in her office before this very minute. All the details here were completely new to me: the cute baby animal posters. The puzzles and the fidget toys. The red geraniums along the windowsill. So there was no reason to feel that the room was *against* me; really, I could tell it was trying hard to *welcome* me.

"Norah Levy?" A tall, plump woman with shoulder-length no-color hair and complicated earrings suddenly burst in and was giving a damp hug that smelled like coffee. *No reason to still be sensitive to smells*, the doctors said. *It's just in your head by now, Norah.*

The woman finally released me. "I'm Ms. Castro, your guidance counselor. And let me say I couldn't be happier to see you back here!"

Which was an odd thing to say, considering she'd never seen me before this minute.

"Thanks. I'm really so glad to be back. Well, not *back*," I corrected myself. "I mean, *back at school.*"

"Yes," she said, fixing large, sympathetic eyes on me. "I can't even *imagine* what the last two years have been like for you."

I nodded. If it wouldn't sound snarky, I'd tell her she was right: *Yes, you couldn't imagine.* But probably better just to nod.

"And how *are* you?" She cocked her head. I knew this question and the head-cock from several moms in our neighborhood. It meant: *But how are you REALLY? You can tell ME.*

"Okay," I said. "Maybe a little tired."

"Oh, and how could you *not* be! With what your body has been through." She shook her head, jangling her earrings. "Well, it's all behind you now."

All behind me. I kept nodding, because what else could I do?

"Although let me give you some advice, Norah: Take it slow. Anytime you need to rest during the day, just go to the nurse's office or come here. Everybody understands! And if they don't, tell *me*, and I'll be happy to explain, all right?"

"Thanks," I said.

But I was thinking: *You haven't said it yet. How could you explain me to anyone if you couldn't even say the word?*

I had CANCER, Ms. Castro. The gods don't zap you with it if you say it out loud.

"It's no problem, Norah, *believe* me." She clasped her hands on her chest. "And you're finding everything all right?"

"Well, my map got me to the guidance office. So yeah." I tried a smile. On the long list of Weird Things I Had to Deal With, one was the fact that while my classmates had been here since fifth grade, I'd spent the last two years either at the hospital or at home. So while I wasn't new to most of the other kids, I was new to this building. Also new to middle school in general, but that was another thing.

"Ah, perfect! So you won't need this map I printed." Ms. Castro swiveled her chair toward her desk, which was crowded with family vacation photos: a bearded guy, Ms. Castro, and three kids hiking, swimming, skating, rafting. All of them flashed big white teeth as they squinted into the sun. They looked like they never even got the sniffles.

"Let's see what other goodies I have for you!" Now Ms. Castro was sorting through a stack of papers. "Oh yes, you'll be happy to hear I've arranged for you to have an elevator key!"

That surprised me, because my legs worked just fine. "What for?" I asked.

"Only to conserve your energy. Your homeroom is up on the third floor, and so are a few of your classes. And the stairs are always very crowded. So this way—"

"Oh, but I'd much rather use the stairs."

"You sure, dear? There's no shame in using the elevator."

"I'm not *ashamed*. I just really don't *need* it."

Maybe my voice sounded too sharp. She blinked at me. "Well, I'll keep the key card here for you, just in case you change your mind."

But I won't, I thought.

Ms. Castro opened a desk drawer and slipped the key card inside. Then she popped a mint Tic Tac into her mouth, offering me one, which I didn't take. How did she not know that kids didn't eat mint Tic Tacs, that they were a grown-up thing? If you're a guidance counselor, you should know stuff like that.

"All right, next item," she said. "On Friday, I had a long chat with your tutor. It sounds like Ayesha worked you very hard, especially in math and science."

Just hearing my tutor's name made me smile. "Yeah, but we

read a lot too. *The Golden Compass*, everything by Rick Riordan, *The Chronicles of Narnia*, the *Enchanted Forest Chronicles*, *Alice in Wonderland*, a whole bunch of Greek myths—"

Ms. Castro smiled. "She says you 'impressed the pants off her.' "

Now I was grinning. Working with Ayesha was the only good thing about the past two years. She was the coolest person I'd ever met, and ridiculously smart. Not only that, but she understood me. She'd been me, or a patient like me, when she was thirteen, so everything I was going through—all the is-this-a-bad-dream-or-am-I-awake stuff—was totally familiar to her.

"Anyway," Ms. Castro continued, exhaling mint fumes, "after taking a long look at your test scores, and considering what you covered with Ayesha, we're wondering if it makes sense for you to start the year in eighth grade math and science."

"Wait," I said. "What?"

"Norah, you've always been an extremely strong student. And it does appear that while you were out"—she said "out" instead of "sick"—"you've completed the curriculums for seventh grade math and science. Don't you think it would be silly to repeat it all?"

"But I don't mind!"

"Well, but *shouldn't* you mind? You're a very bright girl. Why would you want to waste a whole year when you could move forward?"

I couldn't argue, not if she put it that way. Not wasting more time was a big thing with me these days. And moving forward was even bigger.

Still, my stomach was flipping like a caught fish. "But I'm still in seventh grade?" I managed to ask.

Ms. Castro nodded so hard her earrings jangled. "Oh yes, absolutely! All your other classes are with your friends. You're still in a seventh grade homeroom, and you have seventh grade lunch. Just for two classes a day, we'd like to see you move ahead, because the fact is, you've already *gone* ahead. And I have to say, your hard work in spite of your illness inspires us all!"

I didn't work hard on purpose, I replied in my head. *I just did it because—well, what ELSE was I supposed to do with all that time?*

Also: She said "your illness." Still hasn't called it by its name.

"What about my parents?" I asked.

Ms. Castro widened her eyes. "What about them?"

"Did you talk to them? About this moving-ahead business, I mean?"

"We mentioned that we were considering the switch, yes. And I told them that first I wanted to discuss it with *you.*" But she handed me a new schedule, which made me realize she'd already decided everything, even before I walked into this office. "So here you go, then, Norah. You'll be in Ms. Perillo's first period math class and Mr. Hennesy's fourth period science. They're wonderful teachers, very understanding, and they're both aware of your whole story."

My whole story. About the time I was "out."

WITH CANCER. I HAD CANCER, MS. CASTRO. ACUTE LYMPHOBLASTIC LEUKEMIA.

I swallowed. "But I don't know any eighth graders."

"Yes, we considered that, but there are some lovely girls in those classes. Thea Glass is one of our student leaders, and a terrific athlete. And Astrid Williams is head of the Art Club."

Good for them. What does that have to do with ME?

"Norah," Ms. Castro said in a softer voice, "we certainly don't want to pressure you, and we know that coming back after such a long absence will be a challenge all by itself. So why don't we say this: Start the term in these two eighth grade classes, and if you're not comfortable for any reason, we can always switch you. But it would be harder to switch you up a grade than down, so really, it makes sense to start this way. Do you want to try?"

I couldn't think of a way to argue with that logic, so I nodded.

Ms. Castro beamed. "That's excellent! And I'm sure Ayesha will be pleased too. Shall we head upstairs together now?"

"Actually, I'd rather go myself. I mean, I can find the rooms."

"I'm sure you can! Well, you should get going, then. Homeroom's almost over." All of a sudden, she grasped my cold hands in her big, soft ones. "Norah, I want you to feel that this office is your safe place. Whenever you need a quiet moment, or a cup of hot cocoa, the door is open. I'm here for you. We *all* are. *Anything* we can ever do, *please* let us know."

"Can I keep that maze thing?"

"Excuse me?"

I pulled my hand away to point to the toy collection on the small table.

"Honey, with what you went through"—*CANCER! IT'S CALLED CANCER!*—"go right ahead. Take whatever you like—the Rubik's Cube, the Silly Putty, anything!"

"Actually, I was just joking," I said, immediately sorry about my lame attempt at humor. One of the things about cancer: People were always giving you stuff—crocheted hats, balloons, stuffed animals. Like they could make it up to you with a pad of Mad Libs and a Pokémon key chain. And sometimes you had to let them, because you felt sorry for them. I mean, really, what else could they do?

But I didn't feel sorry for Ms. Castro. She had too much loud, jangly energy, and I wasn't even sure that I trusted her.

And now she was eyeing me in a way that made me stare at the carpeting. "Remember what I said, Norah. Stop by whenever, for any reason. And I'll be checking in with you often."

"You really don't have to," I said, stuffing the new schedule into my backpack.

NICE HAIRCUT

My cancer treatment took two years. Most weeks I spent at Phipps-Davison hospital, getting meds "delivered" (that's the word they used) into this tube stuck in my chest. Sometimes, especially when I had a fever or was just feeling extra awful, Dr. Glickstein and Dr. Yorke made me stay at the hospital overnight. Other times I was there just during the day: I'd be assigned a bed in the section they called the "day hospital," and get my meds through an IV while I was resting, reading, watching videos, even doing crafts in the playroom. (Yep, a playroom—the Pediatrics floor had so many little kids they needed a special room for all the Legos.)

When we knew it was possible for me to return to school in the fall, the doctors begged me to wait.

"Just until October first," Dr. Yorke said. "Norah, your immune system has taken quite a hit from all the cancer meds, and we need to wait six months before we can revaccinate you. So if you go back to school right now, you'll be a target for every germ out there. And as we know, schools are germ factories!"

But Mom and Dad insisted I start school in September, along with all the other kids.

"Just like normal," Dad told the doctors.

"As normal *as possible*," Mom said, pretending to smile.

They wouldn't give up, and finally, the doctors surrendered. I guess they realized that after controlling everything about my life for the past two years—what I ate, how many glasses of water I drank, how many times I went to the bathroom—their supreme powers had finally expired.

But just because Mom and Dad had won that battle, it didn't mean things were back to normal for *me*. Because now my parents decreed their own hypernervous List of Parental Back-to-School Rules:

No after-school activities. Just a (healthy!) snack, homework, and REST.

No socializing on weekends, and no sleepovers (until they say so).

Avoid germy kids!! (And remember, all kids are bacterial bipeds.)

No school bus (a virus on wheels).

No school lunch (E. coli-teria).

Use hand sanitizer a billion times a day, especially after touching all concrete nouns.

Avoid the school bathroom unless you REALLY, REALLY have to go. Afterward, scrub hands for two full minutes with soap and scalding water! Do NOT use air blowers to dry hands; use paper towels only. (But if you touch paper towel container, return to Go and repeat all hand scrubbing! For two extra minutes—or until skins falls off!)

Stay home if ANY symptoms: e.g., sneezing, coughing, upset stomach, fatigue, burping, skinned knees, torn finger-nails, cavities, paper cuts, split ends. When in doubt, STAY HOME, preferably hiding under a blanket.

All right, I'm exaggerating, but not a ton. And the truth was, I was so excited about going back to school and having a life again that I would have agreed to anything (*Avoid using the letter e in all sentences!*) So really, none of the Parent Rules was a major problem for me. But it was like they didn't believe it, like they assumed I needed them to recite the rules at breakfast, and then again on the drive to Aaron Burr Middle School.

"If you get tired during the day, just go to the nurse's office," Mom said. "Mrs. Donaldson is our point person at Burr. They called her from the hospital, so she knows *exactly* what to do. And she has a cot set aside just for you, if you need it."

"I know," I said. "You told me that yesterday. Also the day before."

"Well, sorry, sweetheart, but it's really important. You have less stamina than you think."

"I'm not so worried about Norah's stamina," Dad said. "I'm more worried about other kids' germs."

"I'm more worried about their cooties," I said.

Dad laughed. Mom didn't.

"Norah, this isn't a joke," she said, sighing.

Dad winked at me, but I pretended not to see it in the rearview mirror. I didn't want to play Whose Side Are You On. Not this morning, of all mornings.

And now, as I was running up the stairs to the third floor, I found myself wondering if Mom was right: Maybe I didn't have such terrific stamina. My heart was thumping and my breath was short, although possibly that was just from nerves. Because eighth grade math? What if it was too hard? Even with all the work I'd done with Ayesha, I didn't consider myself a math-and-science person. And Ayesha liked me, so maybe she'd over-bragged about how well I'd done.

Also, the thought of classes with the Big Kids made my stomach knot. I didn't know any of them, and they didn't know me. Although, in a way, that was kind of a plus, I told myself: They wouldn't be before-and-aftering me. Except not being with Harper was a definite minus. I wondered what she'd think when I didn't show up in her math class. Maybe she'd worry I was sick again.

"Is this Room 316?" a boy asked just outside the classroom.

"Uh, yeah," I said. "It says so right on the door."

BARBARA DEE

He squinted at the number. "That's a six? To me it looks like a zero."

"It's a fat six," I agreed. "But all the room numbers are sort of fat-looking." Something occurred to me then. "Are you new here?"

He smiled. "Yeah, just moved to Greenwood. I'm Griffin," he added, holding out his hand.

He wanted to shake hands? Was that a thing eighth graders did? I couldn't imagine it was. Maybe at his old school, kids were freakishly polite, but I was pretty sure not here.

Still, I shook his hand. And right away I thought, *I should Purell*. Except that would seem rude. And strange.

"I'm Norah," I said.

"Nice to meet you, Norah," he said. "And nice haircut."

"Thanks." I liked it too, but it felt weird how other people kept commenting. Especially people like Griffin, who didn't realize I used to be bald.

Then I noticed he was holding *Artemis Fowl*, a book I read three times during chemo. And maybe stupidly, I blurted: "Someone told me it's a pixie cut. But not like the pixies there."

I pointed at his book.

His eyes grew. "You've read *Artemis Fowl*?"

"Yeah. It's one of my favorites. Although there are pixies in Harry Potter, too, right?"

He nodded. "Also *Spiderwick*. I think there's some in *Wee Free Men*, too."

I realized I was staring at him. This boy—Griffin—was extremely cute. His reddish hair was spiky and messy in an I-don't-care sort of way, his brown eyes were sparkly, he wasn't too tall, *and he read books*. Good ones too.

I didn't know what else to say after that, so I walked into the classroom. Amazingly, he took the seat next to me.

"I hate not knowing people," he said, as if it were an explanation for his seat choice.

"Yeah, me too," I admitted. "I don't know anyone here either."

He raised his eyebrows excitedly. "You're new also?"

"In a way. More like recycled, actually." Now I definitely needed to change the subject. "Anyhow, if no one knows you, you could have fun with that."

"Yeah? Like how?"

"You could be anyone you want, right?"

"True. I could tell people I'm the human incarnation of the griffin. You know what a griffin is, in mythology?"

One thing I knew was mythical creatures. "Aren't they half lion, half eagle?"

"Yeah. Body of a lion, but head, wings, and talons of an eagle."

I nodded. "In Harry Potter, Dumbledore has one on his knocker. And the name Gryffindor means *golden griffin*."

"That's right," he said, smiling. "I used to have a sign outside my room: 'Griffin Door.'"

"Used to?"

"Yeah, not anymore." His smile flickered. "You read a lot?"

"It's practically all I do." Immediately, I realized how strange that sounded. "Anyhow, you're lucky. I wish my name was a mythical creature, but it's just Latin for 'honor,' which is kind of boring."

Griffin shrugged. "So make up a norah."

"I guess I could. Maybe."

Eighth graders began invading the room then, greeting each other, hugging, laughing loudly. They were enormous, and looked a million years older than me, especially the girls, who had curves and boobs. Some of them had on eye makeup, a few had dyed parts of their hair purple or blue, and most of them were wearing black and gray, colors that didn't even count as colors.

Versus me, with my short brown hair, my teeny size, and my flat chest. I crossed my arms in front of the Cheeto-colored tee, which suddenly seemed to be screaming *GIRLS' DEPARTMENT*, even if it didn't have pandas or ballerinas or ice cream cones.

"Hey, can I ask you something?" Griffin was saying. He seemed embarrassed. "Could I please borrow a pen? I forgot one."

"Oh, no problem." I quickly unzipped my backpack. On the bottom, underneath the binders and folders we'd bought yesterday, was my small sketchbook, and my pen, colored pencil, and marker collection. "Take any one you want."

He peered into my backpack and took out a green gel pen. "Wow, you sure have a lot of writing utensils."

"What?"

"Pens. Pencils. Markers. Why do you have so many?"

Because I spend a lot of time in waiting rooms. "I like to draw. Well, not really *draw*. Doodle."

"Yeah? Can I see?"

It was kind of a weird question to ask someone, but he seemed interested. I mean, not like he asked it to be nice—more like he was actually curious. So I took out my sketchbook and flipped through some pages, showing him zentangles, random swirly shapes, then some dragon-ish creatures I'd invented.

"Those are awesome," Griffin said, lingering over the dragon-ish creatures. *"Really."*

I blushed. "Thanks."

He shook his head. "You should see how I doodle. I'm terrible."

I laughed. "How can you be terrible at doodling?"

"I just am. All I do is cubes. I'm the world's most boring doodler."

"That's silly. I bet if you got yourself some really good pens—"

"Hey, bro, could you please move your desk like two inches?" Some kid was shouting and jabbing my shoulder. It took me a second to realize he meant *me*; *I* was "bro."

Why was I "bro"?

Oh. Because of my short hair. And also my flat chest and orange tee.

I felt my entire body break into a sweat. I couldn't answer this kid. Or move, either.

"What's the matter, you deaf?" the boy demanded. He raked

his long dark hair out of his eyes in a way you do only if you're in love with yourself.

"Are you talking to *Norah*?" Griffin asked the kid loudly. "Just chill, okay?"

Now a very tall blond girl with a pointy nose and too much mascara walked over and pursed her lips at the boy. "Rowan, you're such an idiot. That's a *girl* you were just talking to. You should apologize."

She smiled at Griffin, a smile I didn't like. And she didn't even look at me, even though I was the one she was supposedly sticking up for.

"Sorry," Rowan muttered. You could tell he wasn't even embarrassed by his mistake.

"It's fine," I muttered back.

The tall blond girl didn't take her eyes off Griffin. "Hey, I don't know you. I'm Thea."

Griffin extended his hand again. "Griffin Kirkley," he said, smiling.

Thea giggled in a way that reminded me of the coin return in the hospital vending machines. Immediately I hated her, as well as Rowan. And I almost hated Griffin, too—except right at that moment he dropped his hand from Thea's grip. "This is Norah. She's new here too."

Thea glanced at me. "Hey, Norah," she said in an airy voice.

"Hi." I pretended to search my backpack for something. There was no reason to think Thea knew me from before. But even so, I didn't want her attention, and I was relieved when she finally stopped chatting with Griffin and took a seat on the other side of the classroom.

The class began with Ms. Perillo handing out textbooks, talking about her expectations, her test policy, her homework policy. (Before middle school, did teachers have "policies"? I couldn't remember any.) Then she wrote some problems on the whiteboard. As I copied them into my green binder, I had to admit that this was the right class for me; in fact, they were starting with stuff I'd covered with Ayesha months ago.

But kid-wise? I wasn't sure. Everyone seemed rude or not especially friendly. Griffin was nice, but he wouldn't stay nice, probably, not once the other kids started to notice him. There was no point assuming I'd made a friend, I told myself; I seemed like such a baby compared to everyone else—and obviously he'd realize that soon enough, if he hadn't already.

So for the whole class period I didn't talk to him, or even look at him.

Well, except for when he slipped me a piece of paper on which he'd drawn a stack of cubes.

SEE? he'd written underneath. *WORLD'S MOST BORING DOODLER.*

DOODLES

Norah, what *happened* to you?" Harper cried. "Why weren't you in math?"

Just before the start of second period English, I was back on the second floor, meeting up with Harper outside the classroom. "I got switched to eighth grade," I said. "But just for math and science."

When she pushed her long light brown hair out of her eyes, I could see they were worried. "You did? How come?" she asked.

"Ayesha got me too far ahead, I guess. But it's okay," I added quickly.

"You sure? Wouldn't you rather be with us? I bet if your parents complained—"

"No, no, I really like the teacher." I felt my face tingle. "And anyway, I'll be with you guys for everything else, right?"

"You'd *better* be." Harper searched the classroom as we stepped inside. "All right, so where should we sit?"

Right away I spotted two empty seats next to Silas. Harper knew he was my good friend, so it surprised me that she was even asking the question. "With Silas, of course," I told Harper.

"Um, maybe not."

I looked at her. "How come?"

Harper rolled her eyes. "I think he's saving those seats. One of them, anyway."

"He is? Who for?"

She cupped her hand over my ear. "Kylie. In math, I heard him telling people."

"And *did* she sit with him?"

"Nope," Harper said, making a popping sound on the *p*.

It was hard to process what I was hearing. Silas Blackhurst had always been my neighborhood bike-riding buddy, a skinny kid with scabby knees and a chipped front tooth who shared my taste in bad jokes. The thought of him with a crush on Kylie Shen—it made no sense.

Although, to be honest, I'd sort of lost touch with Silas lately. The whole time I was in the hospital and all the months I was home recuperating, he sent me silly texts and links to YouTube videos. But he never visited. So maybe I'd missed something.

Harper led us over to some empty desks in the back of the classroom, and I sat, never taking my eyes off Silas. When Kylie and Aria walked in the door, his face lit up; when they sat next to this chatty dark-skinned girl named Addison Ventura, his shoulders slumped. Probably everybody could read his body language, even Kylie, if she wanted to. I mean, it was so obvious it was embarrassing.

"Crap," I murmured to Harper. "Poor Silas."

Harper shrugged. "That's how it was first period too."

"Why does he even like Kylie?"

Harper seemed surprised by the question. "Can't you tell? She's really pretty and cool. And fun."

I didn't argue, because I knew that Kylie was *exactly* the sort of girl boys crush on. My problem was that I couldn't see *Silas* being one of those boys. He'd never liked girls before. He'd never even noticed that *I* was a girl. We'd just always been friends: two kids on bikes, patrolling the neighborhood for evil elves. On the lookout for jokes, the dumber the better.

A youngish woman with long brown hair and cherry-red lipstick appeared at the front of the classroom, introducing herself as Ms. Farrell. Instead of teacher clothes, she was wearing black leggings and a tee with the cover of *Alice's Adventures in Wonderland*—and she'd decorated the walls with photos of dogs she'd rescued and given names like Hermione and Frodo. Right away I could tell Ms. Farrell wasn't boring—and when she announced that for our first unit we'd be reading Greek and Roman myths, I was ecstatic.

But not yet, she said. Today she wanted us to write a

paragraph or two describing one thing we wanted people to know about us.

Aria's hand shot up. "You mean it could be anything? Like our favorite pizza topping?"

Ms. Farrell smiled. "It should be something meaningful, like something you believe passionately, or your favorite pastime, or an experience that affected you in some deep way. Something people should know so they get who you really are."

"What do you mean by 'people'?" Malik challenged her. "People in general? People in this room? Or just *you*?"

"Let's say people in this class," Ms. Farrell replied. "But if it's something only *I* should know, please make a note of that, and I'll make sure we don't share it with the class."

My heart sank. This was exactly the kind of assignment I'd been dreading. What could I *possibly* write about myself? *My favorite sport is growing hair. My favorite pastime is resting. I passionately believe in blood donation . . .* I mean, I passionately did NOT want to write a cancer thing. My life wasn't *The Norah Levy Story, Starring Cancer.* And cancer wasn't what I wanted people—or even just one teacher—to know about me.

Okay, but what was? After the last two years, I felt hollowed out, like an old tree trunk.

I peeked around the classroom. People were ripping paper out of their notebooks, sighing, writing, tapping their toes, twirling their hair, biting their fingernails, crossing out words, erasing.

Even Silas, who hated to write anything longer than a text.

And now Harper was eyeing my still-empty page. "Just write anything," she murmured.

"Like what?" I murmured back.

"I don't know. I'm writing about an art project. Write about a book you read."

I groaned. "You know how many books I've read, Harper? It's all I've *done*."

For a second I thought about Griffin, how I almost blew my secret. Fortunately, I hadn't told him something like: *Yeah, for the past two years, I've basically stayed in bed, reading about mythical creatures.*

A hand on my shoulder. When I looked.up, Ms. Farrell was smiling down at me. As soon as I saw that smile, I knew she knew everything. And it was stupid to think she wouldn't have known. Probably all the teachers knew. Even the office ladies and the janitors.

"Are you having trouble thinking of something to write, Norah?" she asked kindly.

See? She knew my name! I didn't tell her, so how else would she know it?

"Yeah, I guess," I admitted.

"Well, try to keep it simple, then," she said. "I always tell students who are having trouble thinking up a topic, or getting started: Just focus on what's right in front of you. Think small, not big."

"Okay, thanks," I said. Ms. Farrell walked away, leaving a fancy-soap smell behind her.

Focus on what was right in front of me? Right in front of me was a purple gel pen. My favorite "writing utensil," as Griffin called it. What a weird expression. Forks and knives were utensils, not pens. Although it was kind of cute he said that. Come to think of it, he'd never returned my green "writing utensil." I needed to get it back from him, which meant we'd have to have another conversation.

And thinking about that cheered me up a little, I guess.

So, just before the end-of-period bell rang, I wrote:

My favorite writing utensil is my purple gel pen. I use it for doodles, which I wouldn't call my favorite pastime, but it does pass the time—haha. What I passionately like about doodling is that it doesn't matter. Nobody asks what your doodles mean or counts them or compares them to last week's doodle. No one wants to know if your doodles are finished, because finishing isn't the point when it comes to doodles. Also, no one tells you that your doodles look better than they do, because who cares what doodles look like, anyway? They're completely private, which is the best thing about them.

LUCKY ME

Mom and Dad pounced on me the second I stepped out of school.

"So how was it?" Mom asked.

"Okay," I said. "Long."

"But good?"

"I guess."

"Norah, are you going to share *any* details?" Dad was smiling, but his eyes weren't.

I shrugged. "I like my English teacher, I think. She said we're doing Greek and Roman myths, so that's cool. Also, I got put into eighth grade math and science, but Ms. Castro said she told you that already."

Mom and Dad exchanged glances.

"No, that's not exactly accurate," Mom said. "We discussed advancing as a *possibility*. But we never officially *agreed*."

"Although we did agree it would be your choice," Dad told me.

"Once we had a chance to talk it over." Mom turned to me, her eyes looking worried through her glasses. "Well, baby, what do you think? Do you *want* to skip ahead? Because we're ready to call the principal if that seems like too much."

"Don't worry, it's not," I said quickly, remembering the last time my parents phoned Mr. Selway. Some hospital people wanted to come to school to explain stuff to the other kids: why I wouldn't be at school for two whole years, what I was doing at Phipps all day, how to visit me, why I had no hair. But Mr. Selway told Mom and Dad he wouldn't allow the hospital people to come, because all that information about me "might upset the students."

"Yes, cancer is 'upsetting' for Norah, too!" Mom had yelled into her cell.

I remember hearing Dad beg Mom to "please calm down for Norah's sake." ("Calm down?" Mom had shouted at him. "Don't tell me to calm down! My daughter has *cancer*!" "So does mine," Dad had answered. And then there was a lot of fierce whispering, just like there used to be before they got divorced.)

I mean, I was mad that the hospital people weren't allowed to come to my school. But it was weird how Mom had thrown a tantrum about it. And I remember thinking: *If anyone should be throwing a tantrum, it should be ME.*

Now we got into the car, which Dad had parked across the street.

"Well, aside from the class switches, how *else* was the day?" Mom was asking me. "Did people bombard you with questions?"

"Not really. I think they were afraid to, truthfully."

"Did anyone say anything really dumb?" Dad asked.

"Well, one kid said he'd heard that broccoli cured cancer. And in music, this girl asked if I knew her aunt, who had leukemia too. Because, you know, all leukemia patients know each other."

Dad laughed. "Yeah, well, you know, old Lou throws a great party. Big guest list."

I laughed too. This was our running joke: Lou Kemia, a cigar-smoking crime boss, was the chief villain of my story. Although sometimes the villain was Luke Emia, a sci-fi warlord with a battalion of white blood cell storm troopers. Or Low-Key Mia, who sapped your energy and kept it in a jar in her evil lab. Or Lucky Me, who used chemo warfare. Dad and I kept changing the villains, depending on what was going on with my treatment.

Mom didn't share our dumb sense of humor, but she chuckled anyway. I knew she was trying her best to do a lot of things for my sake—laugh at our jokes, not argue with Dad, not second-guess the doctors and nurses. She'd even taken a leave from teaching biology at a college out in California, and was staying with her friend Lisa, sleeping on a foldout sofa in Lisa's basement. And here she was in Dad's car, sitting where his girlfriend, Nicole, usually sat, probably noticing Nicole's gum wrappers in the cup holder.

As for Dad, he'd also given up a lot for me these past two years. He was a sports journalist, so he could keep writing articles even when I was in the hospital, but he couldn't travel to away games, obviously. Also, I knew that after he and Mom broke up, he was sad for a long time. But he'd finally starting feeling better again, and things were good with Nicole. So it had to be hard for him to have Mom around again every day, even if they were careful never to fight in front of me.

Mom also had this thing about unbunching towels so they wouldn't mildew, covering toothbrushes so they wouldn't collect bacteria, and rotating things in the fridge so they wouldn't spoil. I guess she always was a bio-nerd, so probably Dad was used to this; but I was positive that ever since I'd gotten sick, she was way more germ-conscious. And I knew she was doing all this towel unbunching and toothbrush covering out of fear, and wanting to protect me—but the thing was, it wasn't her house anymore.

Now it was where I lived with Dad, just outside New York City, about an hour from Phipps-Davison Hospital. When my parents split up three years ago, the plan was for me to switch back and forth between them, spending half the time out in California with Mom, the other half back in Greenwood with Dad. (Yes, I know it sounds crazy. But I was only nine at the time, and totally freaked about the divorce, so I begged them to divide my time like that.) And the sickest part: I spent that whole year wishing for only one thing—that my parents would get back together again. So in a crazy way, I felt like I caused my cancer. Not really. But sort of. A little.

Phipps-Davison is a famous cancer hospital, so Mom never questioned why I was being treated in New York, even though it meant her moving back here for now, sometimes eating meals with us in Dad's kitchen. She was always a very picky eater, and now she was constantly sniffing around the pantry closet, poking at Nicole's spice rack, making almost-snarky comments about how Nicole was a "New York foodie," whatever that meant.

As for Nicole, she tried to keep out of Mom's way, which meant she had to keep away from Dad. Dad never mentioned this, but I could tell her absence made him unhappy. Except what could he do? Whether anyone liked it or not, Mom, Dad, and I were a threesome again, a unit, an unsplit atom of a family.

At least until Lou Kemia kicked us out of his party. And even though I was back at school, back to normal, back to having a life, who knew when that would be?

ALL BETTER NOW

High on the list of Weird Things About the First Day Back: never actually connecting with my old friend Silas. In every class we had together, he made it clear that he wanted to sit with Kylie, not with Harper and me, and at lunch, he sat with Kylie and Aria. Well, not *with* them—more like with a bunch of kids that *included* them. Although as far as I could tell, Kylie didn't even notice he was at the table.

Why was he doing this? In my opinion, he was wasting his time trying to get the attention of someone who definitely wasn't interested in him. Even worse, he was ignoring *me*.

So the next morning, as I ate my scrambled eggs while Dad pretended not to watch me, I decided to talk to Silas before homeroom. I wasn't mad at him, I kept telling myself. And I wasn't hurt, either. I was just confused. Because: *Hello? Remember me?* I mean, of course he did.

I asked Dad to drive me to school early, and he did, without asking too many questions. But what happened was, I was walking upstairs to Silas's homeroom when I nearly smacked into Ms. Castro.

"Norah Levy!" she shouted. "How did it *go* yesterday?"

"Oh, just fine, thanks," I said quickly.

"Wonderful! Math and science classes too?"

"Yep." Stupidly, I was blushing again. This was because Griffin had sat with me in science, too, meaning we were not just tablemates, we were also lab partners.

Ms. Castro probably assumed I was red-faced from stair climbing. "Don't forget, I have that elevator key if you change your mind," she said.

"Thanks. But no, walking is good exercise." As I said this, I remembered the big-toothed, athletic kids in her desk photos; walking up a school staircase was hardly exercise to the Castro family.

She smiled at me. "Well, remember what I told you: Don't push yourself. And we'll have a chat later in the week, okay?"

"Sure." I exhaled, relieved to be done with her.

But she took a step down, paused, and turned to face me again. "Oh, so I hear you've met the new student, Griffin Kirkley!"

"You have? I mean, yes, I have."

"Nice boy. Told you that you'd make a new friend, right?"

I nodded, avoiding her eyes. How did she know I'd been chatting with Griffin? Were there cameras in the classroom?

Maybe the teachers were reporting all my actions to Guidance. *Day One of Cancer Girl's Return: She sharpened her pencil!*

By the time I got to Silas's homeroom, he was already inside. I said hi to Malik, who was in the hall, putting up posters. On one of them, he'd drawn a bunch of crazy angles and written, in big green letters: DON'T BE OBLIQUE, VOTE FOR MALIK. Another one had a picture of a giant wave and said MAKE A SPLASH, VOTE FOR MALIK THRASH. He sure was working hard on these posters, I thought, wondering if anyone besides me even noticed his artwork.

Then I waved through the glass of the homeroom door, hoping somebody would see me mouthing the word *SILAS*. Finally, Addison Ventura waved back and yelled something in Silas's ear. I gave her a thumbs-up, and she made the heart sign on her chest, which had to be a cancer reference, because why else would Addison heart me? The last conversation we'd had was probably in third grade. Fourth grade at the absolute latest.

"Hey," Silas said as he finally stepped into the hall. "Everything okay?"

I nodded. "Definitely. I just wanted to say hi. Because I hardly saw you yesterday!"

"Sorry. First day back is always crazy, so." He did a little laugh-cough.

"Yeah, I guess. You want to eat lunch together later?"

He scratched his nose. "Oh. Sure."

"Great," I said.

BARBARA DEE

We both stood there, not saying anything. Malik finished taping up his posters and walked off.

Then Silas blurted: "So, Norah—you're all better now, and everything?"

I never knew how to answer this. Because the question really was: *SO, ARE YOU GOING TO DIE?* And usually I wanted to answer: *YES, I AM. EVENTUALLY. AND SO ARE YOU, IDIOT.*

But Silas was my friend, so I didn't want to be snarky. "Well, I'm done with chemo," I answered, "but I still have checkups at the hospital once a month, and they're constantly checking my platelets—"

"Platelets?"

"It's part of your blood. It helps with clotting."

"Oh."

"But I'm okay," I added quickly. "They wouldn't let me come back to school if I wasn't."

"Awesome. Well, anyway, I really need to get back. . . ." He waved his arm in the direction of homeroom, like they were solving climate change in there, or something.

"Okay. See you later, Silas. At lunch."

"Yeah, bye," he said, already turning away.

FRIENDSHIP BRACELET

Back when the doctors agreed that I could return to school, they made me talk with the pediatric social worker, a woman named Raina Novak who had a nose stud and a slight accent that she told me was Serbian. I liked her because she was a marathon runner, and showed up at the hospital in neon-colored spandex, like she was just about to go out for a run.

Also, she was always handing out stuff—gummy bears, stickers, jigsaw puzzles—to all the kids on the Pediatrics floor. I guess these were sort of "cancer gifts," but I didn't mind. Once, she even gave me an extremely cool set of markers. "From the Crafts department," she said, putting her finger over her lips, which I interpreted as: *I took them for YOU, Norah, but don't tell any of the other patients. This is our little secret, okay?* I wondered if Raina had "little secrets" with other patients, but even if she did, I always liked her: She seemed like one of the few hospital people you could imagine *outside* the hospital, listening to music in her earbuds while she went running in Central Park.

At first, when the doctors said I needed to talk to Raina, I was afraid that she'd just repeat what they said, tell me to wait another month to "regain my strength." But she didn't.

"Yes, you need to go back to school, Norah," she declared. "It's time."

Which was what I'd been hoping she would say. And yet as soon as she said this, my stomach twisted. "Are you sure? Because the doctors told us—"

"You don't want to go?" She searched my face.

"No, I do! It's just the doctors said an extra month of rest—"

"Right," she said crisply. "Rest is good. But it's more important to start school on day one, with all the other kids."

"Okay, great." It's what my parents had been arguing, so I was used to hearing it. And really, it did make sense to me, even if it also made my insides weird.

"Although I have to be honest," Raina continued, "It won't be easy."

"Oh, but school *is* easy for me! I'm a good student. And compared to cancer . . ." I didn't even bother to finish that sentence. I just shrugged.

Raina smiled. "What I mean is that what we call 're-entry'— returning to the healthy world—can be tricky. Some kids find they're a little behind academically. But in your case, Norah, I think the challenge may be more social."

"What do you mean?"

She offered me a small bag of fancy jelly beans, which I took. "You've been out of school for how long?"

"Twenty-two months."

She tore off the end of her own bag of jelly beans and popped one in her mouth. "Almost two years. That's a very long time when it comes to friendships."

"But my friends are amazing! You've met Harper, right? She's the one who gave me this."

I held out my wrist to show her my purple friendship bracelet. A present from Harper the day I first went into the hospital.

Raina admired my bracelet. "Yes, so pretty. And Harper seems like a lovely girl. Although I haven't noticed other friends here lately." She checked my face.

"Oh," I said. "Well, my friend Nessa used to visit a lot, but she moved to Texas last spring. And some other kids came at the beginning, but . . ." I ripped open my jelly beans and ate one. Buttered popcorn. Yum.

"That's what happens," Raina said, chewing. "When kids get sick, friends pay lots of attention at first. They're curious, they're scared—and a kid with cancer is big news. But sometimes, after a while, the news gets old and the visits stop. That's why it's wonderful to have a friend like Harper."

"Oh, but also Silas! He's a good friend too. My *oldest* friend."

"Silas? I don't think I've ever met him." Raina frowned thoughtfully.

"Well, we used to ride bikes together and make up stories about evil elves. Back when we were little, I mean. And now he texts me and stuff."

"Texting is nice." She nodded. "How come he doesn't visit?"

"I don't know. Hospitals make him nervous, maybe."

"But you're the sick one. What does *he* have to be nervous about?"

I chewed a few jelly beans at once so that I wouldn't have to answer. But I got a funny fruit/licorice combination. Why was Raina saying all this? Was she *trying* to make me feel bad?

She seemed to realize that she'd hurt my feelings, so she patted my hand again. "Norah," she said, "I just want you to go back to school with realistic expectations. Don't expect your friendships to be just like they were two years ago. You've been through something very big here, yes, but your friends have been through their own situations, which are big to *them*. And you haven't been a part of that world."

"But Harper tells me everything! It's not like I don't know what's going on with people!"

"Yes, but it's not the same as being *in* that world. Also . . ." She took a slow breath. "Some of your friends and classmates may be a bit freaked-out by certain aspects."

"Like what?" Although as soon as I asked this, I knew the answer. By my head, which at that point was still bald. By my face, which still lacked eyebrows, making me look like an emoji. And by my skin, which was sort of grayish, the color of a white sock when it gets washed with a bunch of dark clothes. Probably also by my tiny, skinny body, which looked like the body of a malnourished eight-year-old: no boobs, no shape. The fault of the chemo drugs, Dr. Yorke had explained, promising that I'd "catch up eventually."

Raina nodded, as if she realized I'd answered my own question. "Some kids may want to ask a lot of questions, and you're going to have to decide beforehand how you want to deal. It's fine to say something like 'I'd rather not talk about it' or 'It's personal.' What I always tell kids: Just because someone asks a question doesn't mean you owe them an answer. And you don't need to entertain anybody with your cancer story. Even grown-ups." She paused. "Although *not* sharing can be tricky too."

"What do you mean?"

"Just that you need to balance things. You *could* refuse to discuss the topic; I mean, it would be completely understandable. But maybe you want to consider how people would feel about that."

I stared at the carpet pattern, which I'd always thought looked like some kind of alien terrarium: cacti from outer space. The way *other people* felt about my sickness: Why was that my problem? I didn't get why we were even discussing it.

But Raina wasn't finished. "All I'm saying, Norah, is that when the time seems right, maybe you could explain things to people in your own way. Your decision, your words. Just throwing it out there." She shook out the last few jelly beans and popped them into her mouth. "Although my guess is you won't get too many questions. Cancer scares the bejeezus out of people."

I had to laugh at the word "bejeezus," which sounded so American, even with her Serbian accent. "Well, Silas isn't scared," I said.

"I hope that's right. And I hope it works out with all the kids at school." Raina stood. "Shall we go to the lounge? They're doing make-your-own sundaes, and I think we have some cool new stuff at the craft table."

BEST PART OF THE DAY

After talking to Silas, I went to homeroom telling myself: *Well, good, you'll meet for lunch, and everything with him will get back to normal.* Whatever normal was. Because the more I thought about what Raina had said about him in our last conversation, the less sure I felt. All the good stuff about Silas—how we hung out together after school, making up stories, cracking each other up until we fell off our bikes—seemed so long ago. My parents would *never* let me ride a bike now. Because what if I fell off and scratched my knee? Germs could attack my immune system. And then . . . you know. The apocalypse.

I took my seat and opened my sketchbook. But Kylie and Aria pounced right away.

"Norah, we didn't think we'd see you today," Kylie declared.

I looked up at her. "Why not?"

"Kylie said you'd be crazy to come back," Aria said.

"Okay, that's *not* what I said," Kylie protested. "I said after what you've been through, Norah, you should be taking a long vacation somewhere, like on a tropical island. Instead of coming back here, to this." She pointed to Malik and Harrison Warner, who were competing to see who could fake-burp louder. "I mean, seriously, though, if I had what *you* had—"

"Acute lymphoblastic leukemia," I said.

She laughed. "What?"

"That's the kind of cancer I had. It's the most common type of leukemia. They call it ALL for short."

Kylie swung her long, perfect black hair. "Omigod, we don't need all the gory details."

"Kylie, shut up," Aria said, giggling nervously.

"Well, sorry, Aria. But don't you think it's kind of depressing? And anyway, Norah doesn't have it anymore, so."

See, Raina? I just explained it to people. My decision, my words. And look what happened.

"Excuse me, Norah, can I please talk to you for a second?" A girl I knew from before, Cait Gillespie, was standing in front of my desk. "In private?"

"Sure," I said, glad for a chance to escape. I followed her over to the windows. "What's up?"

Cait was twirling her dark reddish hair and gazing at me with slightly bulging blue eyes. "Norah," she said in a quivery voice, "I just wanted to say I'm really so happy that you're back, and I'm sorry I didn't visit you more in the hospital. It was just really, really hard—"

"That's okay," I said quickly.

"I mean, seeing you like that, and all those other kids . . ." Her eyes filled. *Oh, crap. She isn't going to cry now, right?*

I made myself smile. "Yeah, I know. We didn't look so great."

"You didn't *look* so great, you know?"

I just said that. Why is she repeating? "Okay, anyway, it's completely fine—"

"Also, if you need anything—I mean, if I could help you with anything at school . . . ," she said. "Although really, Norah, you're so smart, *you* should probably be helping *me*!" Her nervous laugh sounded like a hiccup.

"Do you need a tutor?" I asked her. "Because I know a great one named Ayesha—"

"No, no, that was a joke! Sorry! It wasn't very funny. Just, you know, if there's anything I can do . . . besides curing cancer." She giggled, her eyes avoiding mine.

"Well, thanks, Cait. I'll definitely ask you."

"Great, Norah. *Definitely* ask me."

"Okay. Um." Was she done? I didn't want to be rude by going back to my seat.

"Well, that's it," she said. "Just, you know. I hope you're not mad at me? And sorry!"

Before I could tell her to please, PLEASE stop apologizing, she ran back to her seat.

"So have you decided on a norah?" Griffin asked. This was right before the start of math, and, except for a couple of girls I didn't know, we were the only ones in the room.

For a second I had no idea what Griffin was talking about. Then I remembered yesterday's conversation about names and mythical creatures.

"Not yet." I opened my sketchbook and drew something swirly. "Although I'm thinking there are probably tentacles."

His eyes lit up. "Yeah, with suckers at the ends."

"Hmm, I don't know about suckers. *Maybe*."

"Well, okay. It's your creature, so you get to decide. Does it swim?"

"Of *course* it does! It's a water creature; why else would it have tentacles?"

"True."

"But I'm also thinking it's a hybrid. So it swims *and* flies."

"You mean it has tentacles and wings? Is that even possible, engineering-wise?"

"Why not! If a griffin is a *flying lion*—"

"Okay, fine, Norah. You can be a flying octopus."

I laughed. "That's not how I'm picturing her! I'm thinking it's more like she changes states—you know, like from sea creature to air creature. Anyhow, I'm still working out the details."

"Cool," Griffin said. He reached into his jeans and took out the green gel pen. For a second I thought he was going to give it back to me, and I wasn't sure I wanted it. I mean, maybe it was stupid, but I *liked* the fact that he had my pen. But then he opened his math notebook and wrote the date. With the green gel pen.

I realized I was staring at his hand, so I opened my own notebook.

And that was when Thea and another girl walked over.

"Hey," Thea said loudly. "*Griffin*. This is *Astrid*."

"Hi, Griffin," Astrid said. She was dressed completely in black and wore eyeliner, which made her eyes look like answers she'd circled on a multiple-choice test. "We were just wondering if you'd signed up for Afterschool."

"What's that?" he asked.

"Oh, you don't *know*? It's the best part of the *day*!" Thea exclaimed. "There are a million clubs you can pick, or you can try out for a team—"

"Thea does volleyball," Astrid said. "*I'm* head of the Art Club."

Well, woohoo for you.

Griffin turned to me. "You should do Art Club, Norah."

"Me?" I croaked, aware that Astrid and Thea were looking me over. "Oh, no. I really don't have time."

"You should *make* time," Astrid said. "It's definitely the best way to meet people, and it's really important to feel involved. Here." She reached into her backpack and pulled out a little booklet: *Afterschool at Burr.*

I pretended to read it. *CPR for Babysitters, Harry Potter Club, Art Club, Hip-Hop, Intramural Track, Chamber Orchestra, Bugs—*

BUGS? Were they serious? How were BUGS an activity?

Astrid was smiling at Griffin. "What do you think *you'd* be interested in?"

He poked his cheek with my green gel pen. "I don't know. Is there a rock band, possibly?"

Astrid and Thea exchanged a glance. I knew exactly what it meant: *Omigod, could this new boy be any cuter?*

"Yeah, actually, there is," Thea answered. "Griffin, you *have* to join! What do you play?"

"Bass. I'm not very good, though."

"Don't be so modest," Thea told him, laughing. She gave his arm a playful little whack. "I bet you're really great."

She does? Why? Because he's cute? I barfed inwardly.

Class started. It was a good thing that Ms. Perillo was beginning with stuff I'd already done with Ayesha, because after that conversation, I was so mad I couldn't concentrate.

THE WHOLE STORY

The next period, Ms. Farrell handed back the paragraphs describing "one meaningful thing" about ourselves. If you got an asterisk, that meant she hoped you'd share it with the class, although it was up to you. Everybody else got a check, which basically meant: *Yes, you turned it in and I read it.* (Ms. Farrell didn't say that's what a check meant, but you could tell by the way she praised the asterisk people.)

About half the class got asterisks, including Harper.

I got a check.

I told myself: *So what. Who cares if she wasn't impressed. It's only the second day of school, and you've dealt with way bigger stuff, right?* But I still felt pretty bad about it. In my fantasy return to school, the teachers raved about my work, just like they always had before. I'd been good at everything, but

Language Arts, or English, or whatever you were supposed to call it now, was my favorite subject, so I was used to getting the best grades whenever I wrote something. And the way Ms. Farrell had come over to my desk—I don't know, it felt sort of personal. Even though she already knew my name, which meant she'd come over to check on Cancer Girl.

For most of the period we listened to kids reading. Aria described her lucky sneakers (she's a runner), Malik explained how he wanted to be seventh grade president, and Harper read about this collage she was making. Then Ms. Farrell praised them for "specificity of detail," explaining the difference between "showing" and "telling," which I already knew.

When class was over, Ms. Farrell stopped by my desk. "I liked your essay, Norah," she said quietly.

"Not really," I blurted. "All I got was a check."

She smiled. "Well, yes. Do you want to know why?"

I nodded, looking at her *Phantom Tollbooth* tee instead of her face.

"Because you didn't show me anything about yourself: 'Doodles don't matter.' You know what I thought when I read it? *Why is she writing this, when there's so much else worth communicating?*"

Like what, for example?

Oh, of course. She wanted a cancer story!

My face flushed. "That *was* what I wanted to communicate."

"That you like to doodle?" She paused for a while. Too long.

Then she said, "Okay, fair enough. But I suspect you're capable of something far more meaningful, Norah."

Was that a criticism or a compliment? Maybe both, and I didn't want to hear it. What right did this teacher have to demand a cancer story? Raina said I didn't need to entertain people, not even grown-ups. And who was Ms. Farrell to decide what was meaningful to *me*, especially since she'd only met me the day before?

"All right, thanks," I muttered, snatching my backpack and escaping the classroom.

The rest of the morning, I tried to put the stupid paragraph out of my mind. And that wasn't hard to do with everything else going on. In social studies, our teacher, Mr. O'Brien, took me aside at the start of class to say that if I ever needed extra time to do an assignment, I didn't even need to ask. This was him trying to be nice, I guess, but the thing was, Mr. O'Brien had an extremely loud, raspy voice, so even though he probably thought he was speaking in a private whisper, the whole class heard. And I was pretty sure I saw Addison Ventura giving me the stinkeye. Like: *Hey, Norah, you're not even sick anymore, so why should YOU get special treatment?*

Also, in PE we were having relay races. The gym teacher, Mr. Ludlow, said I could sit out whenever I wanted, but I told him I wanted to participate. So he put me on Malik's team—which had Addison on it. And when she saw how slowly I ran, even though

I was sweating like crazy, she made a comment to Kylie. Which I heard just the end of: *like a baby.*

So that was how Addison saw me, I realized: a slow-running, sweaty baby who was completely fine now, but got special treatment anyway.

I told myself not to care. *Let Addison think whatever she wants. What difference does it make? She's not even my friend.* But it still bothered me. I hated the thought of anyone deciding I was a faker, that I was using cancer as some kind of all-purpose excuse. *Sorry I farted just now, but you know I had CANCER. Hey, I didn't step on your big toe, it was the CANCER. Can I please have an extra scoop of ice cream? As someone with CANCER . . . !*

I decided not to say anything to Harper about Addison's snotty attitude, though. First of all, because I saw the two of them chatting together at the start of social studies, so obviously Harper liked her, for some reason. And second of all, because as soon as Harper and I walked into the cafeteria, I wobbled.

Harper noticed immediately. "Norah, are you all right? Should I get the nurse?"

"No, no, just give me a minute." I couldn't explain, even to Harper, about the "smell memories," how certain foods (especially fried meat) made me woozy. I knew it was crazy—but after eating hospital hamburgers at the beginning of my treatment, just thinking about them still made me want to barf. And today was Hamburger Day in the cafeteria, apparently. Bleh.

"Anyway," I said, with a cheery all-better-now voice. "Do you see Silas? We're supposed to have lunch together."

Harper's eyes widened. "You are? Oh."

"Is something wrong with that?"

"No. I just never hang out with him anymore."

"How come? Did you guys have a fight?"

"I don't know."

"You don't know if you had a fight?" I searched Harper's face for an answer.

"Norah, look, go have lunch with him if you really want to," Harper was saying. "I'll eat with my Art Club friends. You're *sure* you're okay?"

"Yep. Absolutely."

But the truth was, even though the hamburger feeling had passed, I still felt wobbly—because Harper had never mentioned any weirdness with Silas before. Whenever she'd told me about stuff going on with people—fights, crushes, parties, hurt feelings, new friendships—I always thought I was getting the whole story. It had never crossed my mind that Harper was holding anything back. I mean, why would she? And what she said, that she "didn't know" if they'd had a fight, just seemed strange. Maybe I could ask Silas about it at lunch.

I searched the lunchroom. But I still couldn't spot him, so I figured he was getting his food. I should too, I told myself, even though it meant walking over to where they were making the dreaded hamburgers. *Just keep breathing out. Grab a strawberry yogurt and an apple. Don't look where they're cooking it. Keep moving.*

"Norah, over here!"

Aria was calling me. She was sitting at a big table with a bunch of people: Kylie, Harrison, Malik, Cait, Addison, and Silas.

Wait. *Silas?* Had he forgotten our lunch date?

No, because now he was waving me over. Seriously? I hadn't specified that this would be a private lunch (and honestly, I'd assumed Harper would be joining us)—but why did he think having lunch with *me* meant eating with like half the grade? Especially considering I hadn't seen him up close in almost two years.

Plus, he hadn't even saved me a seat next to him. I had to squeeze in between Cait and Aria, which put me opposite Malik and kitty-corner from Silas. How was this "lunch with Silas"? It wasn't.

"Hi," I said just sort of generally, to everybody. Then I looked directly at Silas, who was eating—guess what. A hamburger. So I had to look away before I barfed.

"Hi, Norah," Kylie replied, like she was the emcee of the table. "We were just talking about what we're doing in After-school. I'm taking Modern Dance and Hip-Hop."

"Oh, cool," I said.

"I'm doing soccer," Cait said. "Norah, if you want, I could show you how to sign up."

With a writing utensil. "Thanks, but I'm not doing After-school this fall."

"Why not?" Kylie challenged me. "Don't you *want* to?"

I suddenly realized that I did. I mean, a lot. And if I could choose anything to join, I'd choose Art Club. Not only to be with Harper—although that would definitely be great—but because Art Club was *where I belonged*, like Griffin said. Even if that snotty Astrid was in charge of it.

But, of course, after school there were the hypernervous Parent Rules, which I didn't want to explain to everyone at the lunch table. "I just have other things to do," I said.

"You mean cancer things?" Malik asked.

"Malik, your *mouth*?" Aria reminded him.

"That's okay," I said as I pulled the foil off the top of my yogurt container and began to mix in the strawberries. When I looked up, everyone was watching me stir my yogurt, like I was Picasso mixing colors.

"Norah, can I ask you a question?" Addison said. "Is your hair short because cancer made it all fall out?"

Aria rolled her eyes. "No, you cheese-head. *Cancer* doesn't make your hair fall out. The *medicine* does."

"Yep," I said. "The chemo drugs."

Addison made a face like someone pinched her from behind. "Omigod, if I lost all my hair, I'd want to *die*."

"No, you wouldn't," Aria said. "If it was a choice between hair and dying, Addison, I'm pretty sure you wouldn't choose hair!"

Although who knew, maybe she would. Addison had a million cornrow braids you could tell were super-important to her. Right up there with oxygen.

"So was it really bad?" Harrison blurted. "I mean, the chemo."

I licked my spoon in straight lines. "Uh-huh. Sometimes."

"I heard the drugs they give are worse than cancer."

"Yeah? Well, that's just stupid."

"So what kind did they give you?"

"You mean, what were the names of all my medicines?"

"Yeah."

"Why do you want to know?"

"I'm just curious."

"Harrison wants to look them up online," Malik teased.

"I do not," Harrison said. But he was blushing.

"Actually, there were so many I don't remember," I lied.

Kylie groaned. "Can we PLEASE change the subject?"

"But it's interesting," Harrison protested.

"Not to me. I think it's depressing." Kylie tossed her shiny black hair. "No offense, Norah."

"I'm not offended," I replied.

Aria smiled at me helpfully. "Anyway, chemo makes people get better. My grandma had chemo for breast cancer, and it made her hair fall out. And she said, *Okay, if I need a wig, it's gonna be a hot one!* So she got this big blond beachy-wave thing. It looked hilarious on her!"

"Norah, did you get a wig?" Addison asked.

"Me? No."

"How come?"

"I didn't want one."

"You just went around *bald*?"

"I wore a hat. People crochet them for cancer patients."

Addison shook her braids. "Yeah? If it was me, I'd totally get a wig!"

But it wasn't. It was ME.

Silence at the table. I peeked at Silas, who was nibbling the corner of a giant cookie. Was he going to jump into this conversation at some point, or just sit there making crumbs? And if he was feeling uncomfortable, was I supposed to rescue him? He was my friend; *he* should be rescuing *me*.

"My uncle had skin cancer three years ago," Cait announced out of nowhere.

"Melatonin," Harrison said.

"No, it's melanoma, actually," I said. "Melatonin is the hormone that makes you sleepy." I stood. "I think I'll get another yogurt. Anyone want anything from the kitchen?"

Fortunately, nobody did. So I walked toward the hamburger-smelling kitchen.

And kept on walking, straight out of the lunchroom.

THE FULL EXPERIENCE

At dismissal, Harper was standing by my locker, waiting for me. "Norah, what happened to you? You weren't in social social studies or technology!"

"I just needed a little break," I said. "So I went to the nurse's office. It's what I'm supposed to do. Nothing's wrong with me, I swear."

"Are you sure? Because you looked weird in the lunchroom."

I laughed. "Hey, thanks a lot, Harper."

I could have explained about the hamburger problem. I also could have mentioned the conversation at the table, how all the cancer talk was making me crazy. But if I said either of those things to Harper, it would just be more cancer talk. Like cancer had turned me into one of those infinite mirrors, where all you see of yourself is a reflection of a reflection, a Rockettes kick line of cancer cells. Talking about talking about cancer . . .

How was that different from actually *being* sick?

The other thing was, even if I did talk about cancer things with Harper, I couldn't be sure of her reaction. Whenever she visited me, in the hospital or at home, we kept the conversation to regular stuff: gossip, crazy parents, favorite web comics, YouTube videos, music. I didn't want to turn her visits into Let's Discuss How Sucky I Feel; I wanted our friendship to stay normal-ish and fun. Besides, even if I *tried* to explain how sucky I felt, Harper wouldn't understand, because how could she? She played volleyball and went ice-skating. Her idea of misery was period cramps.

"I was just tired," I insisted. "And now I'm fine, okay?"

It came out wrong—too fierce, or something. I could tell right away, because Harper flinched. So then of course I felt terrible, because my best friend had been worried about me—not just for wobbling, but for *disappearing*—and here I was, making her feel stupid about it.

But what was I supposed to say? What would Raina want me to say?

She'd say: *That's up to you, Norah. Your decision, your words.*

Which was no help at all. So I changed the subject.

"Can I ask you something, Harper? What's the deal with Silas?"

"Silas?" Harper shrugged. "He's turned into a jerk."

"What happened?"

"Good question."

"No, I mean, did something happen between the two of you?"

She waved her hand like she was brushing away a mosquito. "It's not important. How was lunch?"

"We sat with a bunch of people and he barely spoke to me. Is he mad at me or something?"

"No, I'm sure he isn't *mad*."

"Then why is he ignoring me?"

"Don't worry about him."

"I'm not *worried*, Harper. It's just . . . I don't know. Not what I expected."

As soon as I said this, Raina's other words flashed in my brain: *Don't have expectations*. Okay, but I didn't have "expectations." I'd just thought Silas and I were friends. Even if we didn't ride bikes and battle evil elves anymore.

Harper stuffed some books into her bag. "All right, well, I'm going to Art Club now. Norah, I really wish you'd do it with me. You'd love it, I promise."

"Maybe I will. I'll think about it, okay?"

She blinked.

Oh, great. I've pushed her away again. What's wrong with me?

So then I almost told her about my parents' after-school rule—I almost did. But I stopped myself, because right at that moment, I spotted Griffin out of the corner of my eye.

That night, Dad cooked dinner for Mom and me. The three of us didn't have dinner together every night—which was a good thing, actually. Dad would make some dish that he'd learned from Nicole, so Mom was always criticizing the ingredients—but in a very helpful way, like she was just trying to understand *why* you'd add cilantro, of all things, when regular parsley would work just as well, and was probably cheaper.

When we'd finally sit at the table, they'd both stare at me— or rather, pretend NOT to stare at me—while discussing some topic they'd agreed was safe, like The Crazy Weather We Were Having Lately. If I wasn't hungry, which was most of the time these past two years, Dad would offer to make me some version of his meal, minus the taste. Or Mom would suggest one of her own boring-but-digestible dishes—scrambled eggs, pasta with a dot of butter and a pinch of salt. I'd try to explain that the problem wasn't the food, it was my appetite, and fussing over me was *really not helping*. And they'd explain that they weren't fussing, they were just concerned about my nutrition and calorie intake, and that it was their job as parents, blahblahblah, because they both loved me. And I'd have to say I understood, I loved them both too, and maybe I'd eat a little more in a couple of hours. Although I never did.

When it was just Dad and me, or Dad and Nicole and me, there was definitely way less fussing over my plate. Also, when Mom took me out for dinner at the Greenwood Diner, we usually went for the entire meal without commenting on my appetite. But when I had to eat with both of my parents at the same time, it was like they were competing to see who could take better care of me. And even though they never fought in front of me like Harper's parents did, the way they were both so focused on what I put in my mouth made the whole meal incredibly tense.

Tonight Dad had made some kind of noodle dish with shredded chicken, sliced veggies, and chopped peanuts. It had way too much soy sauce, and I wasn't hungry, but I forced myself to eat wet, messy forkfuls. I even had seconds.

Dad, of course, was thrilled. "Hey, this recipe seems to be a hit!"

"Yep, well, I'm starving," I said. "Because of school, probably."

Mom and Dad beamed. I could see they were both thinking: *Our daughter has an appetite! Praise the gods!*

"So school was good today?" Mom asked.

"Yeah, it feels great to be back!" I stuffed some drippy noodles into my mouth. "Although it would be *so* much better if I could do Afterschool, too."

Mom and Dad exchanged a look.

"Norah—" Dad began.

So then I went for it. "Everybody goes except me, Dad! I feel like there's this whole side of school I'm not getting."

"Yes, and there's a reason for that, honey," Mom said patiently. "We explained to you that at first—"

"I know. You want me to go slow. But did the *doctors* say I couldn't stay for Afterschool, or was that just *your* stupid rule?"

Mom put down her fork. "All right, Norah, that's a little fresh."

"Sorry! It's just that everyone does it except me. It's a very big social thing."

"We know," Dad said. "And we'll be happy to have you participate in a month or so, once you're used to being back."

"Okay, but the sign-up period is *now*. In 'a month or so,' most of the activities will be closed." I didn't even know if this was true, but it sounded true.

Dad and Mom looked at each other. I could see Dad's eyebrow rise just a millimeter, which I interpreted as an opening.

"All right," I said. "What if I went just one day a week? Or two at the absolute most?"

"Norah." Dad shook his head.

"For like an *hour*. Afterschool is ninety minutes, but I'd be fine with leaving after sixty."

"Look, I honestly don't think waiting a few more weeks is such a big—"

"Because really, if I'm going back to school, I should have the full experience." I knew I sounded like I was quoting some parent magazine, and maybe I was. I'd read a lot of stuff in waiting rooms when I wasn't doodling. "Plus, I really think you guys should be willing to compromise."

"Norah," Mom said, sighing. "You've made a very strong case for yourself, and Dad and I hear you, believe me. But right now, we're going to stick with our plan. Go to school, come home and rest, build up your strength, and we'll have this conversation again very soon, I promise."

"We *both* promise," Dad corrected her.

I groaned. "This is totally unfair!"

"Sorry, honey," Mom said quietly, but in an end-of-conversation way.

So I pushed away my plate. Because no sense eating these awful noodles for nothing.

HYDRA

The next morning in math, Griffin noticed the drawing on my hand immediately. "Whoa, what's that? Can I see?"

"It's a Hydra," I said shyly. But I held out my right hand for him so he could see my drawing.

He took my hand and brought it close to his face. "Norah, you're amazing. You just designed this on your own?"

I blushed. "Well, I've been thinking about norahs, and I don't know, I kept having this picture of a Hydra pop into my head. Not the water creature, the mythological one."

I could have told him that after dinner the night before, I was so mad at my parents that I locked myself in my room and spent the evening reading the book Ayesha had given me as a good-bye present—*D'Aulaires' Book of Greek Myths*. She and I had read a lot of myths together, and she knew how much I loved them, especially the one about Persephone in the underworld. Her own favorite was the story of Hercules, how he had to perform a bunch of crazy-difficult labors, including defeating a poisonous nine-headed Hydra monster. Once Ayesha told me that when she had her brain tumor, every time she had to go through another terrible ordeal, like surgery or chemo or radiation, she pretended she was Hercules, which she pronounced HERcules, emphasizing the "her." Anyhow, thinking about Hercules battling the Hydra made me want to draw one, and before I knew I'd done it, I had one on the fleshy part of my right hand, between my thumb and pointer finger.

"Hey, can I ask you something?" Griffin let go of my hand. "Would you draw a griffin for me?"

"You mean . . . on paper?"

"No, on my electric bass, actually. I've decided to do rock band in Afterschool and I think it would look awesome." He was blushing.

"But I can't . . ." I bit my lip. "I mean, I'm not exactly sure what sort of griffin you want. They're not all the same."

"What if I print out a picture and give it to you in science? And then we could meet right before Afterschool, and you could do it then."

"Today?"

"Yeah. We could meet in the music room." He leaned closer to me, so I could smell his breath. A good smell, though, like toast. "The thing is, my bass is really old and in terrible shape, so it needs something to make it look cool. Could you do this for me? As a favor?"

"Sure," I said, before I could think about it too long.

"All right, so here's a question for you," Ms. Farrell said at the start of English. "Why are there myths?"

"To explain things," Aria said.

"What sorts of things?"

"Things that they couldn't explain any other way, like lightning. So they said it was Zeus getting mad and throwing a thunderbolt at somebody."

"Exactly, Aria," Ms. Farrell said. "Can anyone think of another specific myth that explains some natural phenomenon, something we could explain today scientifically?"

Nobody answered.

So I had to. Because it was my favorite myth and everything. "The story of Demeter and Persephone explains why we have different seasons," I said.

Ms. Farrell smiled. I thought she looked extra cool today in her *Where the Wild Things Are* tee and pigtails. "Great example, Norah. Can you tell us the story?"

I nodded. "Well, there's much more to it than this, but basically Persephone was the daughter of Zeus and Demeter, who was the goddess of the harvest. And Hades, who was god of the underworld, fell in love with Persephone, so he kidnapped her and forced her to live in the underworld as his queen. She was really miserable there, and Demeter was so sad without her daughter that all the plants on earth died, and people were starving. But Demeter kept searching for Persephone, and when she finally figured out where she was, she threatened Zeus that she would let everything on earth die if he didn't bring back their daughter. So Zeus sent Hermes to the underworld to tell Hades to let Persephone go. Demeter and Persephone were reunited and really happy again, and everything grew. Then Persephone admitted she'd eaten some pomegranate seeds, which were the food of the dead, and this meant she had to return to the underworld. But Zeus worked out a deal where she could spend half the year in the underworld with Hades and half the year on earth with Demeter. And that's why we have winter and summer."

It was the most words I'd said in a very long time. When I finished speaking, I was a little breathless.

Also, the whole class was staring at me. And Addison had her mouth open, like: *You can talk? Hey, Norah—I didn't remember that about you.*

"Well, that was excellent, Norah," Ms. Farrell said, looking into my face for an extra few seconds. "Yes. Okay. So here's what I'm wondering: If we understand now that the change in seasons is caused by the rotation of the earth around the sun, and *not* by a sort of custody battle for Persephone, why are *we*, in this seventh grade English class, reading these myths *today*?"

"Because it's the curriculum?" Harrison said. Obviously, he

was the kind of kid who thought anything nonscientific was a waste of time.

I raised my hand.

Ms. Farrell turned to me. "Norah?"

"Because they're great," I said. "They're just really great *stories*."

She beamed. "Exactly. They're great stories *still*. Two thousand-plus years later, they hold up. And why is that?"

She was asking the whole class, but nobody was answering. So, without raising my hand, I said: "Because they're incredibly exciting. They're full of action and special effects, like the one where Icarus escapes his prison by wearing these giant wings his dad made him, but he flies too close to the sun and the wax melts. Or the one where Prometheus steals fire from the gods. Also, the one about Sisyphus, this king whose punishment is having to roll the same giant rock uphill every day for the rest of his life. And there's tons of romance, too."

I couldn't say the word "romance" without rolling my eyes a little, but Ms. Farrell didn't mind.

"Yes! That's right!" she exclaimed. "Norah, how do you know so much? Have you read a lot of mythology?"

Yeah, over and over, when I was in the hospital. "A little."

"Well, that's wonderful. You can be our expert mythologist."

The way she said this, it sounded like "expert oncologist." Which I knew wasn't what she meant, obviously. But all gushy praise sounded suspiciously cancer-related.

And, of course, caused Addison to give me another stinkeye.

Then Ms. Farrell started talking about "creation myths," different stories about how the universe was created. It was extremely interesting—although I *also* couldn't stop thinking about my date later today with Griffin. Not that it was a *date* date. It was more of a meeting, an appointment, and I certainly knew enough about *those*. But the way he held my hand when he was looking at my Hydra—I mean, he definitely could have seen my drawing without doing that. So either he was extremely nearsighted or he actually wanted to hold my hand. And the thing was, he didn't even wear glasses.

At lunch, I spotted Harper chatting with Addison and Kylie, so I took a seat by myself in the corner. Immediately, though, Harper came over.

"You can eat with them, you know," I told her. "It's totally fine."

"Of course it's fine," she said. "But I can eat with anyone I want."

"I just meant—"

"I know what you meant, Norah. Don't be silly, okay?"

She nibbled her turkey wrap while I ate my cheese sandwich. Even though I was serious about Harper sitting with Addison and Kylie, the truth was I was glad Harper was sitting with me, glad we didn't need to make conversation.

At least, I thought we didn't. Because all of a sudden she

said: "So what's it like being with the eighth graders?"

I felt myself blush. "Why are you asking?"

"Why? Just wondering. You never say anything about those classes."

"They're okay. I like the teachers. Although Ms. Perillo—"

"I meant the kids. Are they nice?"

"You mean the eighth graders?"

"That's who we're talking about, right?"

"I don't know. Some are. Some aren't."

Harper rolled her eyes. "You were such a chatterbox today in English, Norah. I guess your mouth isn't used to all that exercise?"

"Sorry." I knew I was being too quiet, but there was a reason—and for once it had nothing to do with being sick. Just before lunch, in science, Griffin had given me a drawing he'd printed out, asking if I could do something like that on his bass. In red. It wasn't a super-realistic griffin, more like the type of thing you'd see on a shield. And it didn't have a million details: just the head, wings, and talons of an eagle, the body of a lion. Although the wings would be kind of tricky, especially if he wanted feathers.

"No problem," I'd told him, and he grinned at me.

So now, here in the lunchroom, I was planning the drawing in my head: a side view, I decided. Oh, but wait: All I had were gel pens and pencils. Would they work on the surface of an electric bass? What if they smeared? Griffin had said his bass was black and white, so I could do the art on the white part. But with what?

"Harper, can I ask you a question?" I blurted.

She looked at me over her turkey wrap. Her eyes were so round, I could tell she had no idea where this was going. And with my weird behavior lately, she was probably ready for anything.

"Shoot," she said.

"If you were drawing something on an instrument, what sort of writing utensil would you use?"

"Instrument?" She made a face. *"Writing utensil?"*

"Come on. Pen? Marker?"

"Hmm." She thought. "Not knowing the surface, but guessing it could be slippery, I'd have to say one of those special markers they have in Art Club, because they don't smear. But are we talking about *your* instrument?"

I shook my head. Before cancer, I'd played viola, but I hadn't touched it in the last two years. You couldn't come back to the school orchestra if you were out of practice for two whole years.

"So whose, then?" Harper pressed.

"It's for a kid in math, okay?"

She smiled. "Boy kid or girl kid?"

"Does it matter?"

"No. Although if it's a girl, you just say 'girl.' You only say 'kid' if it's a boy."

"I guess." I took a bite of apple. "Hey, if I came to Art Club, could I borrow one of those special markers?"

"Probably. Pretty sure we have extra. We had them last year, anyway." Harper raised her eyebrows. "You're doing After-school, Norah? I thought—"

"Just for today," I said, and immediately changed the subject.

READY FOR FLIGHT

The only kid in both my eighth grade classes who seemed to remember me from before was Ezra, a pimply boy who could multiply three-digit numbers in his head. I mean, he was a very smart person, but even he didn't seem to remember much. At the end of class that day he walked over to my desk and said, like he'd had amnesia: "Hey, didn't you used to take my bus?"

"Not sure," I mumbled.

"Pretty *sure* you did. Bus three. You always sat with that kid Silas, right?"

Thea was bouncing around Griffin's desk, telling him some dumb, pretend-dramatic story about yesterday's soccer practice, so I doubted he heard Ezra's question, which I didn't answer. But the thought that anyone in our math class knew, or just suspected, the truth about me was horrifying. It wasn't that I cared about my age. I was more afraid that once the eighth graders discovered "my whole story," I'd turn into Cancer Girl for them, just the way I was Cancer Girl for the seventh grade. And if that happened, maybe Griffin would change the way he treated me. Because why wouldn't he? That's how it was with everyone else.

My plan for that afternoon was to get to the art studio as soon as the dismissal bell rang, so that I could avoid bumping into Astrid. I was thinking: *If Astrid sees me with Harper, she might start to wonder where I'd come from, why a "new" kid like me was such good buddies with a seventh grader. And then she might say something to Thea. Who would possibly say something to Griffin.*

When the dismissal bell rang, I ran to the art studio so fast I was panting.

"Can I have that special marker you told me about?" I begged Harper, who was setting up her table. "I really need it now, before people get here."

Harper eyed me. "Everything okay, Norah? You're out of breath."

"I'm fine! I just have something to do."

"You mean 'the instrument,' whatever that is?"

I nodded.

She walked over to a closet and took a black marker out of a jar.

"Wait, can I have a red one?" I asked. "Instead?"

She put the marker back, took a red one, and handed it to

76   BARBARA DEE

me. "Here. I'm not going to ask any more questions, because you won't tell me anything anyway."

Thwack. That felt like a slap. Which I totally deserved. "Harper, I'm sorry. I promise that I'll explain—"

"Whatever. Just make sure you return it, okay? Astrid checks."

"Thanks."

I stuffed the marker into my pocket and ran into the hall. But all of a sudden I realized that I didn't know where to go. Griffin had said to meet him in "the band room," but because I'd stopped playing an instrument, I had no idea where that was. Was "band room" different from "orchestra room"? Maybe it was. I reached into my backpack for the school map.

Just then Thea and Astrid came walking toward me.

"Hey, Nor-*ahh*," Astrid said in a teasing singsong. "So you're taking my advice?"

"Excuse me?"

"Signing up for Afterschool? Like I *said*?"

"Me? No. Well, possibly. I'm kind of checking out something."

"Yeah? What?" Thea asked in that airy way she had.

"Bugs," I blurted. I had no idea where this came from, but it was the only club I remembered from the booklet.

"Well, good. You should definitely do *something*." Astrid said this like she'd decided my problem was laziness, and the only cure for that was swatting flies.

They walked off, laughing. As soon as they turned the corner,

I pulled out the map. The band room was in the basement, so that meant I'd need to find a staircase. And I didn't have time to get lost—probably my parents were already outside, in Dad's car, waiting to pick me up. Well, they'd have to wait a few more minutes. This was definitely more important.

A few minutes later, I'd found the band room. Three boys I didn't know, plus that horrible Rowan, were playing a song I didn't recognize. Griffin was sitting in a corner, watching. When he saw me, his face lit up, and he came running over.

"I was worried you wouldn't come," he said.

"Why wouldn't I? I said I would."

"I thought maybe you'd forget."

"Norahs have supermemory," I said. "It's because we're Hydra creatures. If we ever forget something, we just grow another head."

He laughed. Then he put his hand on my shoulder—which was still so bony I flinched—and led me over to his bass, locked up in a scuffed brown case. "Do you think you could do the drawing fast? The band already has a bass player, so I'm like the sub, but I think they'll want me to rehearse with them soon."

I nodded. "Where should I do it?"

"Not in here." He blushed. "Out in the hall? If you'd be comfortable. I could bring you a chair."

"Sure."

I carried Griffin's bass (surprisingly heavy in its case) out into the hall and waited. A minute later he returned with two chairs—one for him.

My heart banged. He was going to stay out here with me?

"Um, you said you wanted the griffin red, didn't you?" I asked. "You said the bass was black and white, so I thought on the white part—"

"Cool," Griffin said. He unlocked the case and took out his bass. Right away I could see he hadn't been exaggerating. It really was in horrible shape, all nicked and scratched, like something somebody had found at a tag sale for ten dollars. No wonder he wanted a way to distract people.

I pulled out the griffin drawing he'd printed out, but just for making sure I was getting the details right. I didn't want to copy it—it seemed too static, and my plan was to make the griffin seem like it was taking off. Not *in* flight, but getting ready *for* flight, one paw up, the wings arched.

The whole time I was drawing, Griffin didn't say a word, which I was grateful for, because I was already plenty nervous. I drew slowly, because I couldn't erase, and didn't want to smear. Plus, I wanted it to look good.

When I finished, he shouted: "Norah, that's awesome! Thanks so much! It's exactly what I wanted!"

I beamed. And exhaled.

We grinned at each other.

Then he grabbed his instrument and ran inside the band room.

* * *

Just before leaving the building, I checked my watch. It was 3:25. Dismissal was 2:35, so I was fifty minutes late. I'd need to give my parents some excuse: Overslept on the nurse's cot? Review session for a French quiz? Couldn't open my locker? Yeah, that one: and I couldn't find the janitor to help me unlock it.

I smiled apologetically as I got into Dad's car. Mom wasn't there, for some reason. "Sorry," I began, "but my locker wouldn't open and—"

Dad spun around. His face looked scrunched and strangely pale. "NORAH, WHERE WERE YOU?"

I swallowed. "Oh. I mean, I just told you, my locker—"

"Do you realize what time it is? We were frantic!"

"Why?"

"Why? *Why?*"

"Dad, did you think something had happened to me? If anything was wrong, they'd have called you, right?"

"Norah, don't use that tone with me!"

"What tone?"

"The one you also used on us last night, when you called our rule 'stupid.'" He got out of the car and slammed the door. "I'm going to look for your mother."

Not "Mom." *"Your mother."* "Mom *is* here? Where did she go?"

"Searching for you inside the building. Where do you *think* she is?"

He stormed off. I felt dazed. Dad was the relaxed, jokey

parent, the one who never yelled. Why was he overreacting just because I was fifty minutes late? People were late sometimes; it didn't mean they had a relapse of cancer.

It was so unfair. The first good day of my life in the last two years had turned into this. Whatever "this" was.

A few minutes later, Dad showed up with Mom behind him. As soon as I saw her face, I could tell she'd been crying.

Crap.

She got into the car without saying a word, took off her glasses, and stared straight out the windshield.

"Sorry, Mom," I said. I didn't even bother to tell the fib about the locker.

She turned around to face me and exploded into angry tears. It was extremely awkward, because normally Dad would be the one consoling her, but they never hugged each other anymore. So I had to do it, even though she was furious with me and her body felt tight and stiff.

Finally, she pulled away and reached for a tissue in her purse. She honked her nose and put her glasses on again. Then she said: "Norah, don't you do that to us *ever again*."

"What did I do? I'm sorry I was late, Mom, but I didn't do it *to you*."

"Is that what you think? That your safety and well-being doesn't affect us?"

"No. No! I just meant it wasn't *about* you."

"What was it about, then?"

A boy I maybe like. Okay, not "maybe." Like. "I just wanted to check out Afterschool."

"Afterschool?" Dad's eyes were huge. "Norah, are you kidding? We discussed this with you just last night! I thought we'd made it clear: You're not ready yet!"

"Well, I disagree." I folded my arms across my chest.

My parents gaped at me.

"Norah, why are you acting like this?" Mom asked in a quiet, shaky voice. "You've always been so mature and responsible. Even when you were sick, we could always count on you—"

"And you've never treated us with disrespect," Dad added.

"But I *don't* disrespect you!" I protested. "I just wish you'd respect *me*." Now I started crying, too. I didn't see the tears coming; they just snuck up on me. "I'm sorry I scared you, okay? I should have called. But you'd have just told me I couldn't stay, and I *wanted* to stay. And I swear I wouldn't stay if I thought I couldn't. Physically."

"Norah, honey, you may not be the best judge of that," Mom said, handing me a tissue.

"But I'm not a baby!" I shouted. "And anyhow, *it's my body*! Who knows how I feel better than *I* do?"

My parents didn't answer.

So I kept going. "This is so unfair. You guys never *used* to treat me like this! And how come you let me go back to school if you didn't think I was ready?"

Dad sighed. "We do think you're ready. Just not for everything all at once."

"But I'm not asking for *everything*. Only for this *one* thing!"

Suddenly, I spotted Ms. Farrell leaving the building and getting into her car, a small blue convertible three spots over from us. Oh, great: What if she drove past and saw the three of us sitting in Dad's car, shouting at each other, all ragged and sniffly?

"Can we please just go home now?" I begged.

"Gladly," Dad replied, and put the key in the ignition.

SOMETHING I NEED TO TELL YOU

Nobody talked the whole ride home. Did this mean the fight was over? I wondered. It didn't *feel* over, but my parents both seemed exhausted. Dad went into his office "to work on an article," he said (but I saw him in his easy chair with earbuds in), while Mom "rested her eyes" on the living room sofa. I decided to hide out in my bedroom with the door shut. Maybe if we had a break from one another, we'd all calm down, I thought.

Around five thirty, there was a knock on my door, and Mom asked if she could come in. I tilted my laptop away from the door so she couldn't see the page I was reading: Mythical Creatures.

She sat on the edge of my bed, beckoning me to come over for a snuggle. It felt very comforting, actually, especially when she stroked my hair.

"It's growing out, sweetie, " she said. "Although I have to say, I'm a little sorry. That pixie cut looks so cute on you."

"Yeah, I like it too. But I can't wait for my hair to get really long again." I hadn't planned on reporting this, but it just spilled out: "Someone thought I was a boy yesterday."

Mom looked outraged. "You? You look *nothing* like a boy!"

"Actually, I do. Not just because of my hair. Because of my whole body."

"Oh, Norah. Your body's been busy fighting off cancer! You need to give yourself time."

I groaned. It's what she said about everything: *Not now. Later. Wait.* Even for taking bat mitzvah lessons, which you were supposed to do in seventh grade. "A bat mitzvah is not about being a certain age," Mom had insisted when I'd brought it up. "It can happen whenever you're ready." But when, according to her, would *that* be? Five years from now? Ten? Fifty?

It felt like all I ever did was sit in waiting rooms, waiting for things. And after losing two entire years, I just needed everything to happen. Fast.

Why couldn't Mom understand that?

She kissed my cheek. "Not to change the subject, but I wanted to apologize for how emotional I was in the car this afternoon. It must have seemed like a complete overreaction."

"Yeah, it did," I said. "But sorry I was late and didn't tell you."

Through her glasses, Mom's eyes looked red. "Are you *also* sorry you went to Afterschool after Dad and I vetoed it?"

I nodded.

"Okay, good. I think we all need to communicate better. Dad, too." She paused. When she started talking again, her voice sounded tight and a little hoarse. "And as long as we're communicating, there's something I need to tell you: I have to go back to California."

"Wait, what? You *do*?"

Mom blinked. I could see she was forcing herself to stay calm, not get weepy. "Yes, honey. I wish I didn't have to. They've been holding my teaching job for me, but they can't wait forever, so I told them that as soon as you were settled in school, I'd return."

"Oh," I said.

She paused. It was longer than a pause should be. "Don't worry, baby, I'll be back here to see you in just a few weeks. But while I'm away, I need to know that we're all on the same page, and that you're not going to pull something like you did today."

"I promise," I said, swallowing hard. "When are you leaving?"

"I thought I'd fly out after your checkup next Monday. If all goes the way we think it will." She knocked on the wooden frame of my bed to warn Lou Kemia not to try anything.

"Okay," I said in a small voice. All of a sudden, I felt like a toddler on the first day of preschool, desperate to crawl into my mom's lap and beg her: *Don't go. Please. I promise to be good!*

She seemed to read my mind. "Sweetheart, it's time."

"I know," I said.

"Besides, Dad needs to resume his life. I can't hang around this house forever, and that girlfriend of his—"

"Nicole."

"—*Nicole* needs to come out of hiding. It's really not fair to her, and I know they've had dates, but I can tell Dad misses her being part of his everyday life."

I nodded.

Mom cupped my face in her hand. "Hey, be honest with me, honey. You like her?"

"Yes," I admitted. "She's really nice, and she's an excellent cook."

"She's a *foodie*. But if that's what Dad wants . . ." Mom laughed, but right away her face got serious again. "So do I have your word, Norah, that we can trust you? And that you won't simply not show up at dismissal again?"

"Yes! But will you at least *consider* me staying for After-school just one day a week? As long as I'm feeling okay, which I promise to be honest about?"

She sighed. "You don't give up easily, do you?"

I shook my head.

"I'll discuss it with Dad," she said.

"You *will*?"

"Norah, don't get so excited. I just said we'd *discuss* it."

"But what does that mean, that you'll 'discuss' it?"

"It means I say something, then Dad says something, and then I—"

"Haha."

She kissed my hair. "Get off that website and do some homework, young lady."

The next morning in homeroom, I made sure to sit next to Cait, but it was no use. Kylie and Aria came over anyway.

"Norah, I'm having a party at my house on Saturday night, and you're invited," Kylie announced.

"Everyone is going," Aria added.

I peeked at Cait; she was smiling and nodding, which meant she'd been invited too. Phew. She seemed like the type of person who didn't get many invitations.

"That sounds really fun," I said. "But my mom's going back to California, so I think I need to be with her."

Kylie pouted. "Well, will you at least *ask* her if you can come? She'll probably just be packing anyway. And I'm sure she wants you to have a social life again."

Aria gave Kylie a look like: *Uh, maybe that was a teeny bit much?*

But Kylie didn't care. "Harper's coming, obviously. Oh, and your friend Silas, too."

I nodded. But not in a way that meant: *Oh, in that case, count me in!* It was more of an I-heard-you sort of nod. Not agreeing to anything, especially the "your friend Silas" part of

Kylie's comment. Although it made me feel funny that she'd described him that way. Like he was so unimportant I might not remember which Silas she meant.

And why was it "obvious" Harper would be coming to her party? It didn't seem obvious to *me*.

"So how did rock band go?" I asked Griffin a few minutes later in math.

He shrugged. "Okay, I guess. I only played for like five minutes."

"But they liked your bass? How it looked, I mean."

"Yeah. Everyone said it was cool. The drummer especially." Griffin was smiling, but he seemed a bit nervous. "Hey, um. I was wondering: Could you do that same drawing on my hand?"

"On your hand?"

"Yeah, like you did on yours. So it looks like a tattoo or something."

"Sure. I guess. When?"

"Lunch?"

I blinked at him.

"Yeah, I was actually looking for you at lunch yesterday, but I couldn't find you," he said.

"You couldn't?" I broke into a sweat. "Oh, that's because I was in the nurse's office."

"You were sick?"

"Me? *No.* Allergies."

"Oh yeah, I get allergies too. Especially this time of year. And early spring."

"Yeah. Allergies are the worst."

He was looking at me in a way that made my heart bounce. "So can we meet today? At lunch?"

"Oh, sure," I said. "That would be great."

Wondering which period the eighth graders had lunch.

And also how I'd sneak out to get there.

SORT OF HIDING

Before the start of English I asked Harper, who told me eighth grade lunch was fifth period, which was when we had health class.

"Why do you want to know?" Harper asked. She widened her eyes at me.

"Just wondering," I said.

"Norah, *seriously*?"

There was a hard edge in her voice I'd never noticed before. Already I'd had the feeling that she was pulling away a little; not that she was *trying* to make me feel bad, but her casual comments about movies she'd seen with Aria and Kylie, plus the way she kept chatting with Addison, were starting to make me nervous. Harper was too nice to just dump someone for getting sick—but why be friends with a person who couldn't do anything or go anywhere, and totally refused to share information? What was in it for *her*?

When you've switched off the Share Information button for a while, it can be hard to switch it back on. But now I forced myself to speak. "I just need to talk to somebody then. The same kid. *Boy*."

"You won't tell me who?"

"His name is Griffin. You don't know him, Harper. He's a new eighth grader. And we're just friends. Not even."

"Well, but if you're meeting him for lunch, that sounds like friends."

"He likes how I draw. It's not a big deal."

"If it's not a big deal, why skip a class? You'll get in trouble."

"No, I won't. Anyhow, I'm allowed to skip classes."

"If you say so." She gave a sigh. "Hey, are you going to Kylie's party on Saturday? She told me she invited you."

Shoot. "Um, maybe not."

"How come?"

"Mom's leaving for California on Monday."

"And?"

"And I should be with her. It's her last weekend here."

"Okay, so just come for a little while, then."

"I can't."

Harper threw me a look. "Really? Your mom wouldn't understand that this was the first party you've been invited to in forever, and that *I'll* be there, and also Silas, not that you care, plus all your other friends? She wouldn't let you come for like an hour?"

No, because it's against my parents' Back-to-School Rules. I'm trying to get them to change the No-Afterschool rule, so I can't ALSO ask them to bend the No-Socializing-on-Weekends rule!

"Harper and Norah, are you with us today?" Ms. Farrell asked sharply. Class had started sometime during our conversation, and we hadn't even noticed.

"Sorry," we both muttered as we opened our notebooks.

And when Harper passed me a note—*Your mom will be happy that you have a social life again!*—I just wrote back: *I don't know. Maybe.*

Would I really do this? Skip a class my first week back at school? Just to make Griffin believe I was an eighth grader? It seemed crazy, so unlike me, or the person I thought of myself as being.

But maybe I wasn't that person anyway. Maybe chemo had zapped that person right out of me. Or maybe I was still that person *mostly*, but I'd also changed over the last two years. Mutated into a norah. And this tentacled, many-headed creature was the kind of person who met a boy for lunch when it wasn't even her lunch period.

I *had* to do this, I told myself. There was just no choice. If I didn't meet Griffin for lunch, he'd realize that I wasn't in his grade, and then everything about me, "my whole story," would be exposed. Anyway, I'd only be skipping health class—and if there was one class I felt entitled to skip, it was that one.

Because, I mean, all I'd done for the last two years was obsess about health. *I am utterly SICK OF HEALTH. Time for a new topic!*

At the start of fifth period, my heart was pounding as I went up to Ms. Nargesian, the health teacher. She was at her desk, counting pamphlets called *Making Sensible Decisions. That is definitely NOT a message to me from the gods*, I told myself. Even so, I looked away.

"Um, I think I need to go rest this period," I told her.

Right away her eyes clouded. "Of course, Norah! I'll write you a pass for the nurse's office."

She did it on a hot pink Post-it, which I crumpled and stuck in my jeans pocket. To get to the door I had to walk past Harper, who wagged her pointer finger.

I ignored her and went straight to the lunchroom.

What I hadn't counted on was that Griffin would be sitting with other eighth graders—and that these eighth graders would be Thea, Astrid, and Rowan. I couldn't imagine just squeezing into the table with the four of them, and having Astrid and Thea quiz me about the Bugs Club, or watching Rowan check out his hair in his phone camera, the way I saw him do during math.

So I grabbed a napkin and drew a Hydra on it. *Meet me by the yogurt*, I wrote. Then I walked over to Ezra, the boy who'd remembered me from the bus, and asked him to give the napkin to Griffin.

"Why can't you do it yourself?" Ezra demanded. He squinted suspiciously.

"Because we're playing a game, and I'm sort of hiding," I said.

The funny thing was that this made sense to him. He took the napkin and walked over to Griffin's table. I could see Griffin say something to his tablemates and immediately spring up, like a piece of toast popping out of a toaster.

"Hey," he said as he spotted me by the yogurt shelf. "Don't you want to come over? I saved you a seat."

"Thanks, but no. I can't draw in front of people."

"Oh. No, I get that. I can't play bass in front of people either."

"You can't? How can you do rock band, then?"

He winced. "Yeah, it's kind of a problem. But I'm working on it. So where should we . . . ?"

I pointed to a small, empty table near the exit. As we headed toward it, I tried to ignore the people looking at us, probably wondering why Cute New Boy was walking behind Tiny, Skinny New Girl with Short Hair.

"So," I said as we sat side by side. "Your hands aren't greasy, right?"

He shook his head. "Thanks for doing this, Norah."

"No problem." I'd always hated that expression; why had I just used it? "Left hand or right?"

"Well, I play left-handed, so left."

"Me too. I mean, I don't *play* anything, but I'm left-handed."

"Yeah, I noticed."

"You did?"

"Uh-huh. Lefties always notice other lefties."

I didn't know what to say to that, so I concentrated on the drawing. My hand was trembling a little, but I managed to do the griffin, this time from memory. And I had to admit it looked good—if anything, better than the one on Griffin's bass.

When I finished I told him to use hand sanitizer instead of soap and water if he needed to clean his hands.

"Hand sanitizer?" he repeated. "They have some at school?"

"I don't know, but I have a whole bottle in my locker, and I always carry some in my backpack. See?"

When I showed him the small plastic bottle, he gave me a funny look. And right away I realized I'd almost blown it. Again.

UNEXPLAINED ABSENCE

Once I'd finished Griffin's griffin, there were fifteen minutes left until the start of sixth period. I didn't want to go back to health (especially not if they were discussing Sensible Decisions), and there was no point going to the nurse's office for a fifteen-minute nap. Besides, I liked the nurse, Mrs. Donaldson, who had a warm smile and calm blue eyes. If I showed up at the end of fifth period, she might urge me to skip sixth period too—and I already felt guilty enough about missing health.

What I did was hang out in the first floor girls' bathroom. I had it all to myself, so I spent the time staring at myself in the mirror. Was my hair really growing in, or was that just Mom being supportive? It was hard to tell, but maybe it was a *teeny* bit longer. And was it the same color as before? Ayesha had told me that after chemo, her hair grew in darker and kinkier.

Maybe the norah creature would have long tendrils. That could be awesome, actually.

Just before the bell rang, I obeyed the Bathroom Rule, washing my hands with fake-flower-smelling soap, and drying with paper towels. Not that my parents would ever find out if I used the hand dryer—but right at that moment it felt like maybe I owed them some obedience.

At dismissal, Dad was in a great mood. His editor had liked some article he'd written about a baseball player so much that he'd assigned him a longer piece for the magazine—the kind of assignment he hadn't been able to do since I'd been diagnosed. Maybe there'd be a little traveling involved, "but just overnight," he said quickly.

Mom, who was in the car, turned to him then. "Who'll stay with Norah?"

"Nicole," he answered. "I already asked, and she already said yes."

Mom didn't reply. But I knew what she was thinking: *Time to head back to California.* I gave her an extra-big hug when we dropped her off to do some shopping.

When Dad and I got home, we went into the kitchen for my after-school snack. Right away I noticed that the answering machine for the landline was blinking.

"Probably my editor," Dad said happily as he hit the button.

"BEEP. Hello, Mr. Levy? This is Janice Castro, Norah's

guidance counselor from Aaron Burr Middle School. I'm calling about an unexplained absence. Please give me a call as soon as you get this message. I'm here today until four. Thanks very much. BEEP."

Dad eyed me. "Do you know what that means? 'Unexplained absence'?"

My throat closed up. "Not really. I had a pass for the nurse's office fifth period. If she means *that*."

"Well, we'd better check. Don't go anywhere." He dialed the school while I pretended to eat carrot sticks dipped in hummus. "Hello, Ms. Castro? Greg Levy here. Fine, thanks. Just got your message. Yes . . . Today? When? . . . Oh. That's very strange. Are you sure? . . . Oh. I see. Well, no. No, I appreciate that. . . . Yes. Yes, I agree. And her mom will too. Absolutely. Yes. Thanks so much. See you then."

He hung up.

My heart skittered.

Dad turned to me with a confused expression. "You told your health teacher you were going to the nurse's office, but you never went?"

I nodded. "How . . . did she know?"

"Because your health teacher was worried about you. So after class she went to the nurse's office to see how you were doing. And you weren't there."

"Because I wasn't tired! I'm only supposed to go there when I'm tired, right?"

"Uh-huh. So where did you go, then?"

I swallowed. "To the girls' bathroom."

"Why?"

"To look at my hair. There's a really great mirror there, and—"

"Norah. You were in the bathroom checking your hair *the whole period*?"

"To see if it was growing! I *hate* looking like a boy!"

"First of all, you don't. That's just ridiculous. And second of all—why would checking your hair take an entire class period?"

"Because in health they were discussing Sensible Decisions! I *hate* that class! It's torture! I wish I didn't have to do it!"

"But you do. As long as you're in seventh grade."

"That's the problem, Dad! I don't feel as if I'm *in* seventh grade."

"Why not? You mean because you're in eighth grade math and science?"

"No, it's not about that. And I *should* be in those classes, anyway." I chewed my lip. "It's more that there's all this *stuff* happening and I'm not part of it."

Dad gave me a stern look. "Norah, we're not having the Afterschool fight again, right?"

"Why can't we? Mom said you'd discuss it."

"And we will. Just not this very minute. We're talking about you missing a class. On purpose."

"Well, it's not even *just* Afterschool, anyway. There are parties—"

Dad blew out some air. "All right, Norah."

"This weekend, for example. And I can't go! Because you and Mom won't let me!"

Dad sank into a chair. "Norah," he said tiredly. "We're not discussing the Weekend rule *or* the Afterschool rule. We're discussing the fact that if you're back at Aaron Burr, you can't pick and choose which classes you go to. You have to go to *all* of them, unless you need to rest. That's the *only* reason you're excused, and the *only* place you're allowed to be is the nurse's office. Capeesh?"

I nodded.

"Good." He exhaled. "So what's this Ms. Castro like? Mom and I have to meet her tomorrow."

"She wants to see you?"

"Yep. Is she scary?"

I rolled my eyes. "No. She has Silly Putty."

"Slinkys?"

I shook my head. "But a Rubik's Cube."

"Yeah? Well, this should be buckets of fun, then."

SILLY PUTTY

ll day on Friday I tried hard not to panic. But the more I thought about it, the more I couldn't understand why Ms. Castro needed to see my parents. If you skipped a class, you were supposed to get detention. Calling parents into school was really serious, an overreaction. Unless someone had spotted me in the lunchroom with Griffin and I was in trouble for Impersonating an Eighth Grader. Or for Vandalizing a Student's Hand. Or maybe Astrid had reported me to Ms. Castro for Theft of Special Red Marker. Which I should definitely return to Harper right away, I told myself.

I was so obsessed with these thoughts that I barely registered when Silas came over to me at the start of social studies.

"Um," he said. "Hi."

"Hi, Silas," I answered flatly. "What's up."

"Nothing. I was wondering if you were coming to Kylie's

party. She said she asked you but your mom said no."

"Kind of," I said. I really had zero desire to be having this conversation, especially when, for all I knew, my parents could be sitting in Ms. Castro's office right at this moment. Plus, I was still mad at Silas. "Can I ask you something? Why do you even care?"

Silas looked shocked. "Me? What do you mean?"

"Because you've barely even spoken to me since I've been back. I tried to have lunch with you and you basically ignored me."

"Oh. No. That wasn't what I—"

Then I kept going. "And you know else I've been wondering, while we're on the subject? How come you never came to see me in the hospital? I mean, the texts were funny, but it would have been nice if you'd have shown up in person. I wasn't there for a broken leg, you know?"

"Yes, I know," Silas said in a choky voice. "I feel really bad, Norah. I *felt* really bad. But I just couldn't. I'm very sorry."

"Yeah, well. You may be sorry. But you're also not my friend, obviously."

His face turned pink, and his eyes scrunched up. I realized he was in danger of violating the number one rule for seventh grade boys—WHATEVER HAPPENS, DON'T CRY ON SCHOOL PROPERTY—but I told myself that if he did, it was his problem. Because why should I worry about Silas? *I* was the one who'd been sick, not him—just like Raina said.

Class started. From across the room, I could see how his shoulders drooped.

SO WHAT? I yelled at myself. *Do NOT feel sorry for him. It was good you finally told him how you felt. Raina would be proud!*

A few minutes later, Harper passed me a note: *That's why I had a fight with him—because he refused to visit you when you were sick. I didn't tell you about it because I thought it would make you upset. What a jerk.* ☹

At the start of seventh period Spanish, Señorita Coleman said that Ms. Castro wanted to see me. I thought maybe my parents would still be in her office, playing with the Silly Putty, but when I got there, it was just her.

She smiled, a red lipstick smear on her teeth. "Please have a seat, Norah. I met your parents today, and we had a nice chat. You're so lucky to have them in your corner."

I nodded. Were you supposed to tell people about lipstick smears? I'd read something on this subject in one of those waiting room magazines, but maybe that was just for spinach.

"And they both expressed concern about your staying for Afterschool," Ms. Castro added.

Now I focused. "You talked to my parents about *Afterschool?*"

"I did. I explained that I thought it was important—that doing Afterschool would help you feel a part of the Burr community. So we worked out a deal: To start the semester, you can do one day a week."

"I *can*?"

"As long as you're feeling up for it. We don't want you risking your health. But yes."

I was so happy I almost leapt out of the chair to kiss her cheek. But fortunately, I stopped myself in time. "Thank you so much!"

Ms. Castro smiled and nodded, shaking her huge scribble-scrabble earrings. "You're very welcome, Norah. Your parents and I *also* agreed that we'd like to see you open up a little more."

Now I stared. "What . . . do you mean?"

"Well." She clasped her hands in her big lap. "I've heard from several teachers that you've been a bit closed off."

"Ms. Farrell?"

"Several teachers," she repeated, like she couldn't divulge top secret information.

That stupid paragraph. Just because I wouldn't write "My Cancer and Me" on command.

"So I'd like to propose something, Norah. Every year at Burr we dedicate a week to a program we call Overcoming Challenges. We invite in folks who've faced various types of difficult circumstances. And we were wondering if perhaps you'd like to share with the school community about your own challenge. With your health."

You mean with CANCER? I swallowed. "No. I wouldn't like that, actually."

"Oh." Ms. Castro swished her earrings. "Can you tell me why not?"

Because I'm not Cancer Girl. I'm a norah. Who may or may not have tentacles. "I just want to go to school and stay for Afterschool like everyone else, and not keep talking about all that stuff."

"Even to reassure some of your friends?"

"Reassure them about what? They can see that I'm back at school. I wouldn't be here if I were sick!"

"Okay," Ms. Castro said quietly. *She's disappointed, but that's not my problem. Raina said I don't need to entertain anybody with my cancer story, not even grown-ups.* "Well. Will you let me know if you change your mind?"

"Sure," I said. *But I won't.*

At dismissal, Mom and Dad were still dressed up in their meeting-with-Norah's-guidance-counselor outfits. I suddenly realized that this was the second-to-last day they'd both be picking me up from school. On Monday, they'd come here together one more time, we'd go into the city for my checkup, and then Mom would fly back to California. The *don't-go* panic started to bubble up in my chest again, so I yelled at myself to stop.

"How was it with Ms. Castro?" I asked. "Did you guys play with the Silly Putty?"

Before they could answer, I threw my arms around them in a family hug. And they let me do it, even though it smushed the two of them together. "Thanks for letting me do Afterschool! Really, thank you guys so much! I *promise* not to overtire myself! But I'm *not* doing that Overcoming Challenges thing!"

"No one's forcing you," Dad said, smiling.

"It was just an idea," Mom said, as she kissed my hair. "No pressure, honey."

Ms. Castro was right: I *was* lucky to have them. And when I thought about how I'd lied—not telling them the truth about meeting Griffin at lunchtime, and even worse, getting away with it—I suddenly felt like the worst daughter in the world.

WHAT YOU SAY

I don't even remember the rest of that afternoon. I was so wiped out from the week that as soon as I got home I flopped on my bed for a quick nap—and woke up at nine thirty that evening, hungry and headachy. I wasn't even totally awake when I staggered into the kitchen.

Nicole was sitting on a stool, reading a cookbook. She really *was* totally food-obsessed, I thought, although I'd never admit that to Mom.

But as soon as I walked into the kitchen, she looked up at me and grinned. I liked her long dark hair with its silvery threads, and the gap between her top teeth, how she'd never had it corrected. "Hey, girl. Have a good sleep?"

"Yeah. I didn't mean to sleep that long. It was like I passed out."

"You wouldn't have slept like that if you didn't need it. A full week of school is a lot to get used to."

"I guess. Where's Dad?"

"Meeting a deadline." She pointed to his office, which had a closed door. "You hungry?"

"Starving, actually."

"Yay. I made chicken pot pie, whole wheat bread, fennel salad with heirloom tomatoes, and a blueberry cobbler for dessert."

I had to laugh. "You made all that just now?"

"Nothing else to do in this house with your dad working and you snoring away." She got up to serve me. A while ago, I gave up protesting whenever she prepared a plate for me; Dad told me I was being rude, that Nicole actually *liked* serving people her food. And since she couldn't be over here that much when Mom was around, I always tried to be extra-considerate.

As usual, all the food was incredible. Warm, comforting, not too spicy or too bland. If Nicole did all the cooking around here, I'd probably ace caloric intake.

"This is amazing," I gasped between forkfuls.

"Glad you like it. And I love to see you with an appetite."

It occurred to me that I had one. Not a fake one either.

She broke off some bread and added it to my plate. "So how are things going? I feel like I haven't seen you in ages."

"Yeah, because you haven't," I said, mopping up some of the chicken liquid with the bread crust. "It's going okay. Although it's just the first week, so."

She snorted. "You're expecting to fall off a cliff?"

"Well, you can't be sure."

I got cancer, didn't I? Stuff happens.

When I finished eating, Dad finally came out of his office (which he called his "writer's cave," only half jokingly). Nicole brought the blueberry cobbler into the TV room, and the three of us watched a sci-fi movie about cyborgs taking over the earth.

It was a cozy night. We all shouted things at the TV screen, had seconds on the cobbler, and nobody told me to go to bed (probably because I'd had such a long nap). It did make me feel a little guilty to enjoy hanging out with Nicole—but I reminded myself that it wasn't *her* fault that Mom and Dad had broken up. Also, it was great to see Dad so relaxed and jokey again, especially after being called into school for my misbehavior.

The next day, a rainy Saturday, was more rest for me. Nicole disappeared when Mom came over, sniffing around the kitchen the way she always did after Nicole cooked. Dad got grumpy (but pretended to be cheerful) and locked himself in his office again. For the first time I found myself wishing Mom would just leave already so that the house would be less tense. And then immediately hating myself for wishing Mom would leave.

"I booked my flight," she told me. "Monday night out of JFK. As long as your checkup on Monday is completely normal." Then she knocked three times on the table leg.

The two of us played a bunch of board games we didn't finish—Risk, chess, Star Wars Monopoly. We shopped online for non-orange school clothes. She showed me a few knitting stitches (not that I'd ever knit). I dozed with my head in her lap while she did a crossword puzzle. For dinner we ordered Chinese food, and Dad joined us. (They did their best not to comment on my food intake, although when I sneezed once, they both freaked.) Afterward, Dad went back into his office, and Mom and I watched *The Devil Wears Prada*, me cuddled up next to her like a cat.

A boring day, but a good one. And the last mother-daughter Saturday we'd have for a very long time.

On Sunday morning, Harper called.

"You didn't show up last night," she said.

"To what?" I asked.

"Kylie's party. Remember?"

"Yes, but I never told her I was going. Or you. I only said I *might*, because my mom is leaving on Monday."

"So you actually asked your mom? And she actually said no?"

"It's a little more complicated than that." As I said this, I realized it was. Because it wasn't just that Mom and Dad had this rule about me resting on weekends. It was also that I really *had* needed some one-on-one time with Mom before she left. And the reason *why* I did was one of those cancer things that a noncancer person wouldn't understand.

But Harper didn't even ask what I meant by "complicated." Maybe by now she'd given up on me explaining things to her.

There was a too-long pause.

"So what's going on today?" I asked, trying to sound casual.

"Not much," Harper replied. "Just going to the mall with a few people. Aria's getting her ears pierced, Addison wants a new hoodie, and Kylie needs shoes."

I swallowed. "Okay."

Harper must have heard something in my voice, because then she said, "Norah, *please* don't be jealous, okay? They've been really nice to me. The whole time you were sick, they invited me places. I don't know what I would have done without them."

I thought about Addison's stinkeye and Kylie not wanting to hear my "gory details." My throat felt tight, but I tried to sound cheery. "Hey, no, that's really great. I'm not jealous, I'm *glad* for you, Harper."

Another pause. Then she said: "I'd ask if you want to join us, but something tells me you wouldn't."

It's not that I wouldn't. It's that I CAN'T.

"Well, have fun at the mall," I said.

"You too," Harper said. But only because it's what you say.

That evening, I texted my tutor, Ayesha. I'm not sure why I suddenly needed to talk to her— but maybe it was because the conversation with Harper had left me wobbly, and Ayesha was always the one person who understood everything. Everything I was feeling, I mean. Because she'd felt it too.

Me: Hey. Just wanted to say school's going great!

No answer, so I did some science homework. Doodled a zentangle seahorse, then a snake.

Finally, two hours later, my phone chirped.

Ayesha: NORAH! Yay, so happy to hear from you!! They put you in 8th grade math??

Me: Yep. And science.

Ayesha: Bec you're a math/sci nerd like me!! :P So are they hard?

Me: Nah. And I like the teachers. But not as much as YOU.

Ayesha: Yeah I spoiled you forever, haha.

Me: You did!! But I like having classmates again. I think maybe. Mostly.

Ayesha: Yeah, classmates are cool. Maybe. Mostly. ;) How are yr parents?

Me: Ok. Still nervous but . . .

Ayesha: Well, that's normal I guess. So are mine & its been 10 yrs since I was sick haha!! Hey, N, gotta run, meeting my girl-friend. Take care of yrself, work hard, stay in touch, kay? <3

BAD HAIR DAY

Monday morning, I was still feeling tired, but I wasn't about to admit it to my parents. If I did, they'd just make me skip morning classes to rest up for the afternoon checkup at Phipps. But then I wouldn't see Griffin, and that was the one thing I'd been looking forward to all weekend.

And it was good I made it to math, because as soon as I took my seat, Griffin asked if I'd be going to Afterschool. There was "something important" he wanted to ask me, he said.

"Um, I can't," I said. "Not today."

His face fell. "How come?"

"Doctor appointment. For my allergies."

"Oh."

"But I'll go tomorrow," I added quickly.

His face lit up. "Awesome."

I stared at my math notebook. What could Griffin need

to ask that had to wait for Afterschool? It couldn't be that he wanted to go out with me, right? I desperately hoped not. For one thing, I didn't feel ready for that. And for another thing, how would I answer? *Oh, I'd love to, but I'm never available on weekends until further notice for reasons I REALLY, REALLY don't want to talk about*? Maybe all he wanted was to ask was if I'd help him with math; we were having a quiz next week, and I could tell he was kind of lost.

Whatever it was, I'd just chosen my one Afterschool day of the week: Tuesday. I was really looking forward to Art Club because I'd get to hang out with Harper—my only chance to be with her outside a classroom. Unless things had gotten too weird with us—yesterday's phone call was definitely awkward, or something. I probably needed to apologize. Or explain things better. Or just explain things *more*.

"Norah?" Ms. Perillo had written a problem on the white-board.

My brain scrambled.

"Twelve," I blurted.

"Nice." She wrote the number 12 next to the problem. "Rowan, can you explain Norah's answer?"

I smiled and silently thanked Ayesha.

Mom and Dad signed me out of school at ten thirty that morn-ing. As I got into Dad's car, I was super-jittery. This was strange, because all I'd done for the last two years was get scans and tests, so after a while I stopped worrying about them. I mean, having checkups was *what I did*. But maybe the fact that I was starting to have some kind of a normal life made me focus on this afternoon's appointments in a different way.

"Ready, Freddie?" Dad asked. It was what he always said when we were leaving the house for Phipps. Or when a needle was about to go in. Or when a scan was about to happen and I needed to lie still.

"Yep," I answered. "Let's *do* this thing." My line.

Mom turned around from the passenger seat to kiss the air in front of me. Then she smiled, but I could see in her eyes that she was struggling not to cry. This worried me. Because if she got weepy before we were even on the road to Phipps, how would it be afterward, at the airport, when we needed to say good-bye? Assuming everything was okay with me and she could leave, knock on wood.

Dad put on the radio. Traffic and weather on the eights. The stuff normal people cared about. Then sports.

We arrived at the hospital at eleven forty-five. Pediatrics was the whole seventh floor. We took elevator C—and as soon as we arrived on seven, a funny feeling washed over me, like I was safe at home after a long, rocky voyage. It was so strange: When I was here every day, all I wanted was to escape, return home, return to school, return to my life—and my first minute back, I felt a sense of relief so strong it was like my bones all melted.

And right away, three nurses from the day hospital came

running over to greet us, smothering me in hugs, exclaiming about how great I looked, touching my hair. Esme at the reception desk grinned as she asked if I had "fever, cough, cold, or rash," or had "been to a foreign country in the last month." When she wrapped the paper identification bracelet around my wrist, she confessed that I looked so grown-up she hardly recognized me. This had to be what she said to all the kids when they'd finished chemo, because I hadn't "grown up" in the past month at all. But I still liked hearing it.

We took seats in the waiting area. Dad read e-mails on his phone, the way he always did when he needed to shut out the hospital. Mom went to the snack room to get herself a coffee. And a cup of milk and a doughnut for me—glazed, if any were left; otherwise, cinnamon. We knew how everything worked here: how they only had free doughnuts on Mondays. Where to sit for the best wifi. How long we'd have to wait to see our team of doctors and nurses. It was all so familiar, a routine we'd memorized when everything around us was a blur.

But today, for some reason, I didn't take out my sketchbook. Instead, I watched the other kids in the waiting area. Some were just sleepy babies in strollers, their parents so freaked they were barely speaking, or else laughing and chatting superloudly, pretending that if they treated this whole thing like a crazy dream, maybe they'd wake up soon. There were also grumpy, bald teenagers with earbuds, trying to ignore their moms. A goth-looking girl with a shiny black wig. A boy with a college tee and a laptop, giving dirty looks whenever a toddler started shrieking. And, of course, plenty of kids my age: a girl wearing a blue crocheted hat and glitter nail polish. A boy with a Batman baseball cap and a deck of Magic cards. A girl with a bandana and a BAD HAIR DAY tee, curled up in her chair with *Percy Jackson's Greek Gods*.

All these kids seemed sick, I thought: quiet, tired, flattened. Not like me.

And when the girl with the bandana looked up from *Percy Jackson*, I smiled at her. "Great book," I said.

She blinked as if I were speaking Martian.

"Here's your doughnut, Norah," Mom was saying brightly. "Lucky you, they had one glazed left."

Lucky me. I took it from her, hiding it in the napkin. I couldn't explain it then, but I felt guilty about eating it in front of all these kids. Even though my short hair might have communicated: *I was sick like you not very long ago. And look at me now, pigging out on junk food.*

"Norah Levy?" Esme called out. Mom and Dad turned to me, startled. We'd all settled in for the regular wait. Maybe checkups worked differently once you weren't a patient anymore and you had real things to do in the real world.

She led us to Dr. Glickstein's office. Nurses and nurse practitioners and assistants I'd never spoken to before all smiled at me as we walked down the brightly lit hallways to Dr. Glickstein's office. I wondered if they were smiling because they could see I looked better—or if they'd always smiled at me and I'd just been too sick to notice.

"Norah Levy!" Dr. Glickstein shook my hand at his door, the way he always did. It was a joke, a this-is-how-grown-ups-behave handshake. His eyes twinkled behind wire-frame glasses. "How's it going out there?"

"Pretty good," I said.

"She's been back at school a full week," Mom explained. "And exhausted all weekend."

Dr. Glickstein gazed at her as if she were across the street. This was another thing he did: treating my parents politely, but making it clear that *they* weren't the patient, and he wanted to hear from *me*. "Any of those rotten kids cough on you, Norah?" he asked as he took out his stethoscope.

"No. And no one sneezed on me either."

"Let's keep it that way. You'll get re-immunized six months after chemo—until then, avoid germs, please, kiddo, and scrub those hands throughout the day. How's the appetite?"

"Uneven," Dad said.

"*Fine*," I corrected him. "But I'm still super-aware of smells. Especially when there's meat." I stuck out my tongue.

"That'll fade. But maybe you'll always have a thing about Big Macs." Dr. Glickstein winked at me. "There are worse things. Let's see your weight."

I stepped on the scale.

"Up three pounds," Daphne announced, beaming. She was

one of my favorite nurses, always interested in my drawings.

"Is that enough?" Mom asked. "I mean, is she gaining at the right rate?"

"Norah's gaining at the right rate *for her*," Daphne answered.

Something about the way Daphne said that decided me. "Um, can I ask a question?" I said. "In private?"

"You mean you want to talk to *the doctor* in private?" Mom repeated, as if she wasn't sure she'd heard right.

"Yes, actually," I admitted.

Mom's cheeks turned red. Dad's mouth made a small O. The truth was, I wouldn't have minded for Mom to stay, but no way was I going to talk about this in front of Dad. And for me to ask Dad to leave—that would seem like choosing sides, which I refused to do.

"Absolutely," Dr. Glickstein said with a calm smile. "Mr. and Mrs. Levy, would you mind stepping out in the hall for a moment?"

"It's Ms. Lewis now," Mom snapped. "*Dr.* Lewis, actually." But she walked out of the exam room, with Dad right behind her, not even throwing a glance in my direction. Were his feelings hurt? Were Mom's? This was the first time I'd ever asked to speak to Dr. Glickstein privately, and probably I should have warned my parents back in the waiting area. Although if I had, they'd have totally freaked. I mean, they were still both capable of freaking over a single sneeze.

Dr. Glickstein closed the door. "What's on your mind, Norah?" he asked kindly.

I chewed the inside of my cheek. "I was just wondering about . . . uh, about my body. When it'll catch up. To other girls my age."

"Ah. Do you remember when we discussed this?"

I shook my head. Sometimes on chemo I was a bit foggy-headed, and afterward forgot about certain conversations. It was embarrassing, and also a little scary.

"Well, Norah, the chemo does have certain side effects you'll be experiencing for a while. Most girls your age who've been through cancer treatment don't develop at the same rate as their peers. But you will catch up eventually. And you'll get a period, too, never fear."

I shrugged. "I don't care so much about *that*. It's more about how I look. Compared to everyone at school, I'm just so . . . little-girlish. And with my hair so short—"

"Hey, your hair is adorable." Daphne smiled. "And your body is still recovering, honey. You'll get there."

"Okay. Thanks." It was what Mom had told me, but coming from a doctor and a nurse, it just sounded more believable.

Dr. Glickstein asked if I had any other questions. I shook my head.

He chuckled. "Okay, so can we invite your parents back in, before they both have heart attacks? Because I skipped class the day they taught CPR in med school."

"Haha," I said. *Skipped class. That's so funny.*

THE SOCIAL THING

After the exam I had a bone marrow aspiration so they could check me for any leukemia cells hiding deep inside my bones. (Even after two years of treatment, I still hated needles worse than anything, and this one hurt like a whole hive's worth of beestings. But at least it was over pretty fast.) Then I had an appointment with Raina while my parents sat on separate couches in the waiting room, reading their phones.

Raina seemed happy to see me, but a bit distracted, like she'd just run a tough marathon. I guessed she'd had a hard time with some patient.

"So how's school going?" she asked.

"Fine," I said. "And you were right! I mean about the work not being hard for me."

She grinned. "Not surprising, smartypants! And the social thing?"

"Yeah, so you were right about that, too. Silas *is* a jerk. He's practically ignored me the whole week."

"I'm sorry to hear that, Norah. But maybe over time—"

"And I'm still good friends with Harper, but I can't do a bunch of things, and I don't want to keep *explaining* everything to her, you know? Or talking about cancer stuff, which makes me feel guilty, because she thinks I'm hiding information. Which I sort of am, I guess."

"Hmm."

"Plus, she's hanging out with these girls who aren't my friends. They're not my enemies or anything, although Kylie says it's depressing when I talk about being sick and Addison acts like she thinks I'm faking. But I guess since I wasn't around for two years, Harper decided she needed new friends. Which I totally understand, but . . ." I shrugged.

Raina nodded thoughtfully. "Norah, let me ask you a question. Is there someone at school to talk to?"

"You mean someone like you?"

"Yes. Not necessarily a counselor. Any adult, really."

"Well, there's my guidance counselor, but she's kind of bossy. She wants me to do this stupid Overcoming Challenges thing where I have to stand up in front of the entire school and talk about cancer." I shuddered. "Which, by the way, she refuses to say. She just keeps saying I was 'sick' or 'out,' never that I had leukemia, or even just cancer. And it really, really bothers me!"

"That does sound tricky," Raina agreed. "Did you tell her how you feel about that?"

"No, but I'm sure she can tell."

Raina took a small box of Skittles out of her pocket and handed it to me. "So here's a thought: I wonder if you'd be interested in joining a support group at the hospital. It's for kids who've returned to school but are still patients at Phipps."

"You mean come back to Phipps—"

"Just once a week. After school. For support."

"No, that's impossible," I said immediately. I could fast-forward to the conversation with my parents: *Norah, you can't do BOTH the support group AND Afterschool. It's too much! So for now, why not put Afterschool on hold, and later, when you get your strength back—*

Raina chewed some Skittles. "Why is it impossible?"

"Because I have other stuff to do."

"Like what?"

"After-school stuff. Plus homework! And I need to rest."

"Norah, it's only one afternoon a week. And it's on Fridays, so you don't need to worry about homework."

That made it sound doable, I had to admit. But the thought of coming here every week? It would feel like a giant step backward. And seeing all those sick kids in the waiting room every time—I just couldn't. No matter how comfortable it felt when I stepped off the elevator, I didn't belong here anymore. I didn't *want* to belong here.

"I *can't*," I said. "I'm sorry."

The catch in my voice seemed to take her by surprise. "Well, will you at least think about it?" she asked.

I nodded. But of course I wouldn't.

EARRINGS

As soon as we were in the car on the way to the airport, Mom asked if I'd "gotten all my questions answered today." By that, I knew she meant: *I can't ask what you talked about with Dr. Glickstein "in private," but will you at least tell us the general topic?*

So I said the general topic was Hair.

"You couldn't discuss that in front of us?" Dad asked. *"Hair?"*

"Well, it's embarrassing." That wasn't a lie. "Also, I wanted to ask them about ear piercing."

That wasn't a lie either—at least technically. Because ever since my phone call with Harper yesterday, I *had* wanted to ask about ear piercing. I was thinking that with long, swishy earrings like Ms. Castro's, nobody would mistake me for a boy.

The quick way Mom was breathing, I could tell she was

trying not to freak. "Norah, honey, ear piercing is a parent decision, not a doctor one."

"Yeah, I know. But I wanted to hear if *they* were okay with it before I asked *you*."

"Why? Because you assumed I'd say no?"

"I thought you'd say I could get an infection or something, so I should wait. And I'm sick of waiting for everything! That's all I do! Wait, wait, wait!"

"Okay, I'm lost," Dad said.

Mom huffed impatiently. "Greg, we just need to get on the Whitestone Bridge—"

"I know how to get to the *airport*, Janie!! I mean, what does ear piercing have to do with *hair*?"

"I just think I would look a lot better if I could wear earrings," I explained. "At least while my hair is short. And they do it—the piercing—at the mall. Harper went with Kylie and Aria yesterday—"

"Hold on," Mom said sharply. "Norah, I'm about to get on a plane. This is *not* the time to bring up ear piercing at the mall!"

"But why? I don't even need you to come with me. I could go with Harper. Or Dad."

"Not me," Dad said. "Not my department. Sorry."

Then I made a bad mistake: "Or with Nicole."

"*No*," Mom snapped. Her face went red. "You can do it on your birthday, Norah. With *me*."

But my birthday wasn't until April. "My hair will be all grown in by my birthday! I won't *need* earrings then!"

"I'm sorry, Norah, but I just can't think about this right now! We should have had this conversation yesterday. And I really do *not* want another fight with you just before I get on the plane!"

The car went silent. Dad put on the radio: traffic and weather on the eights, then sports. I stared out the window for a while, then took out my sketchbook to draw some norahs.

When we finally got to the airport, Mom had passed from mad-at-me to sorry-she-yelled-at-me. "Baby, I'm going to miss you terribly," she said as we hugged. "But you can call me anytime, day or night. You know that, right? And we'll Skype."

"Sure," I said. "That'll be great."

"And I'll be back here to see you in three weeks! Maybe we'll do the ear piercing then, all right? Would you like that?"

"But my hair will be *longer* in three weeks."

"Norah, honey . . ." Her eyes filled. She didn't seem annoyed with me now. Just sad. Sad for everything.

And suddenly, so was I. All of it—the divorce, the cancer, Mom leaving—was just totally unfair.

"Sorry, Mom, I was just teasing," I said quickly. "Yes, I *would* like that. I love you."

"I love you too, baby. Be good, and listen to your dad."

"I will."

I'm sorry I brought up the earrings like that. I wish I were nicer—a better patient. A better daughter. And sorry I said I'd

do it with Nicole. You're my mom—of course I'll do it with you.
Please don't go.

But then she left, because it was time, and she had to.

That night, Nicole cooked us dinner. It was really good (pasta with vegetables; brownies for dessert), but after Mom took off, I guess I wasn't feeling very hungry. So while Dad and Nicole watched a movie in the living room, I curled up in bed with *D'Aulaires' Book of Greek Myths* and opened to the story of Persephone and Demeter, how Demeter never rested until she got her daughter back from Hades. I knew there were other stories about moms and daughters, but right then it was the only one I felt like reading.

SPIDER-GIRL

The next morning, Griffin was late for math. Ms. Perillo frowned as she reminded him of the rule: Late three times and you get detention.

He waited for her to turn to the whiteboard, then leaned over to me. "You coming to Afterschool today?"

I nodded.

"Can you meet me in the band room?"

"Griffin? First you show up late, and now you're talking?" Ms. Perillo was definitely annoyed. "Do I need to change your seat?"

"No. Sorry," he said. But as soon as she turned away, he raised his eyebrows at me. Same question, I guessed.

Yes, I mouthed.

He grinned, and I willed myself not to blush.

Before English started, I told Harper I'd be staying for Afterschool on Tuesdays, and was doing Art Club. She seemed thrilled—she even gave me a hug—so I knew the weirdness between us wasn't permanent. Which was a huge relief.

But then she said: "Only one thing. The girl who runs Art Club is *horrible*."

"You mean Astrid? Yeah, I know her from math class."

Harper made a barf face. "She *hates* me. We're doing sketches for these murals we're supposed to put up in the halls. I'm supposed to do one for the Overcoming Challenges thing, but everything I draw, she says it's not 'public art,' or she doesn't think it 'communicates,' or something."

"I'm sure your drawings are great, Harper."

"She's all like, 'This is my club, and I'm in charge, so you have to do what I say.'"

"Well, if I do Art Club, I'll stick up for you," I said.

"If? *If?*"

"*When* I do Art Club."

"Yay!" Harper clapped her hands and did a crazy little jig.

For a second, it felt like everything was back to normal between the two of us. It wasn't more Harper taking care of poor Norah; this was Norah taking care of Harper. First time in two years! Woo!

But then Kylie and Aria spoiled it all by walking over. Over to Harper, to be exact.

"Wanna go out for lunch?" Kylie asked in a pretend-evil sort of voice. Her dark eyes were sparkling, making her even prettier.

Harper gave her a crooked grin. "What do you mean by 'out'?"

"You know. Out of the building."

"What? You mean leave the *school*?"

"Don't be such a baby. It's just crossing the street for a slice of pizza, then coming straight back."

"Yeah, but—"

"Come on, Harper. Lunchroom pizza tastes like microwaved dog poop."

"Harper, you'll get in trouble," I murmured. "And for a stupid slice of pizza? It's totally not worth it."

Aria nodded at me. "I told Kylie the same thing, but she's not listening to me, either."

Kylie snorted. "That's because you're boring, Aria. So is Norah. *Harper's* not boring. *Are* you, Harper?"

Harper did a combination laugh/sigh. "Can I please just think about it, Kylie?"

"Only if you think fast. Addison's coming, and we'll be in the first-floor girls' room at the start of lunch. And we're not waiting."

She and Aria went into English.

"You're not *actually* thinking of going with her, are you?" I demanded.

Harper shrugged. "I told you, Norah, we're friends."

"That doesn't mean you need to follow her around like a little lamb!"

"Who says I do? Besides, I didn't say I'd *definitely* go."

"You didn't say you wouldn't."

"Norah, just stop, okay? Kylie's fun. And I really hate it that you're jealous."

"I'm not *jealous*! I just don't get what's so great about her."

Harper looked right into my eyes. "You want to know? She *tells* me things, okay? I know her *feelings*. And I don't have to beg her for information."

In English, Ms. Farrell was talking about how the ancient Greek gods and goddesses were constantly falling in love, cheating on spouses, being jealous, having babies, breaking up, getting revenge, then doing it all over again with someone else. On the whiteboard, she'd even made a giant multicolored chart about all their love affairs, with Zeus almost always in the middle, cheating on Hera with some random female.

"It's like a bad soap opera," Harrison complained.

"I think it's cool," Kylie protested. "More interesting than *some* things we could be studying."

"But you have to admit it's kind of trashy. I mean, for a religion."

Ms. Farrell laughed. She was wearing Harry Potter glasses and a maroon scarf that wasn't Hogwarts, but close enough. "Yes, Harrison, I suppose that's fair. Why do you think so many of these stories are about love and passion, especially the messy kind?"

"So people want to hear them?" Aria guessed.

"But not everyone," Addison insisted. "My parents have been married for like twenty years, and *they* don't cheat. So like, if *they* were ancient Greeks, why would *they* want to hear about gods who cheated?"

"Fair point," Ms. Farrell said. "Why *would* they? Any ideas?"

Malik raised his hand. "Maybe it's not about the gods acting better or worse than regular people. Just bigger."

"Bigger how?"

"Just in every way. Like that guy who was in love with himself, what's-his-name?"

"You mean Narcissus?" I asked.

"Yeah, him," Malik said. "It's not like he's a *little* conceited; he's so in love with himself that *all* he does is stare at his own reflection in the water. And then that nymph, what's-her-name?"

"Echo?" I said.

"Right. She's so in love with *him* that all she does is follow him around, repeating his voice. Until she's nothing but a voice." Malik made his hand fall over and smack the desk. "It's regular emotions, but bigger."

"Interesting," Ms. Farrell said. She waited. "Any other ideas?"

I couldn't stay quiet. "I think we're supposed to feel that the gods are like movie stars. And you know how when you see a movie you identify with the hero, even though the hero is a beautiful, famous actor? I think we're supposed to think the gods *are* bigger and stronger and more emotional than us, and we're *also* supposed to identify with them."

Addison laughed in a nasty way. "Yeah, Norah, so who do *you* identify with? Wait, I know—how about that Spider-Girl?"

"What Spider-Girl?" Malik demanded.

"You know, Arachne, the braggy girl who made everyone pay attention to her weaving all the time. Until finally Athena got sick of it and turned her into a spider."

Harper frowned. "I don't get what that has to do with Norah."

Addison swished her braids. "I just meant because Norah likes attention. The way Arachne did."

My insides froze. It was like I'd swallowed a block of ice.

"Whoa," Harper said. "Addison, you did *not* just say that."

Addison blinked. "What's wrong? All I said was—"

"Yes, we all heard what you said," Ms. Farrell cut in. "And I'd like to assume—I'm *going* to assume—that you didn't mean how it must have sounded to Norah." She walked over to her desk, like she was changing the channel. "Okay. Norah was saying before how we root for certain gods and goddesses, not because we think we're on the same scale as they are, but because we see ourselves in them, or feel connected to them somehow."

Harrison waved his arm. "Okay, but what if we *don't* feel connected to any of them?"

Ms. Farrell peered at him over her Harry Potter glasses. "Oh, I certainly hope that's not true. Because if it is, you're going to have trouble with our first big project."

KRAKEN

When it was lunch, I didn't look for Harper. If she was sneaking out of the building for a dumb slice of pizza, I didn't want to know about it. Because it was a stupid thing to do (versus sneaking into eighth grade lunch to meet Griffin, which was something I absolutely *had* to do). Plus, it meant hanging out not only with Kylie, whose idea of "fun" was getting in trouble over melted cheese, but also with Addison, who'd just called me a show-off in front of the entire class. And based on what? The fact that people wouldn't stop commenting about my cancer? Like she thought I *wanted* people to pay attention to that, when the truth was *exactly the opposite*. The whole thing was insane. *She* was insane.

I took a seat at the table I'd shared with Griffin. After a couple of minutes, Cait came over.

"Okay if I join you, Norah?" she asked shyly.

"Sure," I said. I moved my napkin so she'd have room for her sandwich. Not a hamburger, thank goodness.

She sat. "Can I say something? I thought what Addison said in English was really mean. You didn't deserve it."

"Thank you."

"I don't know why she said that."

"It's almost like she's jealous."

"You think she's jealous?"

Yeah, Cait, I just said that. "I don't know. I really don't understand. It's crazy to be jealous of someone for getting sick."

"Yeah, really crazy," Cait agreed.

I nodded. We both ate our lunches. Cait wasn't much of a conversationalist, but she was a nice person, I had to admit.

All of a sudden, she looked up and blurted: "Can I ask you something? You know that eighth grader Rowan, right?"

"Yeah, he's in my math class. Why?"

"I don't know. I was just wondering what he's like." Now she blushed.

"Why?" I asked. "You *like* him?"

"No. I don't know. Maybe."

Should I tell her what I thought about Rowan? But how could she not see it for herself? The way he was always fussing with his hair—it was kind of obvious, wasn't it? Maybe you weren't supposed to tell people that their crush was a conceited jerk, like how you weren't supposed to tell people they had red lipstick smeared on their teeth. Or maybe this was more of a spinach-in-the-teeth situation, where if you *didn't* say something, *you* were the jerk.

Just then Malik came over to us. He looked upset. "You guys seen anyone messing with my posters?"

"What posters?" I asked him, glad not to be talking about Rowan.

"I keep putting up posters for the election, and they keep getting taken down."

"Why would anyone do that?" Cait said.

"Good question." Malik shook his head in disbelief. "No one's even running against me."

"So why are you putting up posters, then?" I asked.

"Just so people know there's an election and vote. Last year like twenty kids voted. *In total.* Sometimes I wonder why I'm bothering," he grumbled as he walked off.

A minute later Harper showed up. She took the seat next to me without saying a word. I didn't want to advertise her stupid pizza outing to Cait, so I just asked Harper if she'd "accomplished her mission."

"I didn't go," Harper admitted.

"You didn't?" I could barely contain my excitement.

"Yeah," Harper said. "I stood in front of the girls' room waiting for Kylie. Addison never even showed up, but guess who did. *Silas.* I swear, he's so in love with Kylie he'd follow her anywhere. And I refuse to hang out with that traitor. So." She shrugged.

"How is Silas a traitor?" Cait asked.

"To Norah," Harper said. "For never visiting her at the hospital."

Cait's face crumpled. "Oh. But I didn't either."

"Well, but you apologized, at least," I said quickly. "And explained about it, which Silas never did. And anyway, Silas was always one of my best friends. But since I've been back, he barely even talks to me."

"That's so weird," Cait said. "Do you know why?"

I shook my head.

"Traitor," Harper pronounced.

I turned to her. "Okay, but *you're* friends with someone who insulted me in English class."

"You mean Addison?"

"Who else?"

"Actually, Norah, I told her off right after English. I said if she said anything like that again, I'd never speak to her. Again. *Ever.*"

"You did? Well, thanks."

"You're welcome."

The bell rang.

"Oh crap, I didn't get any lunch," Harper said. "Norah, I'm taking your apple, okay?" Before I could say yes, she grabbed it and started chomping.

At dismissal, I told Harper I'd meet her in the art studio for Art Club, but I had "something to do" first. She didn't ask what it was. But I took a deep breath and words tumbled out: "I need to meet that boy I told you about, Griffin. And I think I may like him, but there's nothing going on between us, just this little art project. And I'll be right back."

"Okay," Harper said, smiling a little.

I ran down the stairs to the band room. Cait was sitting on the floor outside the open door, singing along as Rowan played Nirvana. The funny thing was, her voice was louder and stronger than it ever was when she was talking. As soon as she saw me, she sprang up, blushing hard.

"Isn't he great?" she said. "I wish I could play an instrument."

"I'm sure you can, if you really want to," I said.

She shook her head. "I took guitar lessons for a few months, but I was so bad the teacher quit on me."

"Well, what about singing? I heard you just now—you're good!"

Her eyes bulged. "No, no, I'm the worst singer ever, Norah! I mean, I *love* to sing, but I'm terrible—*Oh*. Excuse me!"

Griffin had come out into the hall, causing Cait to race off.

"Hey," he said to me, smiling.

"Hi," I answered. "I can't stay long; I'm doing Art Club."

"That's awesome, Norah. You *should* do Art Club."

I smiled back. "You wanted to ask me something?" I reminded him.

"Right. So the band really likes the griffin drawing. And we were wondering. Um."

"Yes?"

"Well, if you'd maybe design a sort of band logo. Since you're amazing at drawing creatures."

"Oh. Well, thank you. But—"

"We're called Crackin'."

"Excuse me?"

"You know. Like the beast."

"Oh, you mean *Kraken*? Like the sea monster?"

"Yeah." He smiled shyly. "The name was my idea."

"Cool. That's a really good band name."

"You think so?"

"Definitely. And it goes with Hydra." *Erg. Why did I say that? What a dumb thing to say!*

But Griffin nodded. "I guess that's what made me think of it: giant sea monsters, squids, tentacles. But with suckers, so not like norahs."

"Right. *Totally* not like norahs."

"Anyway." He seemed a bit confused. "So . . . would you do some sketches? And then we'll pick one?"

"Sure." I held out my hand for him to shake. "It'll be fun."

And then something terrible happened: Instead of shaking my hand, he gave me a hug.

GIRL TALK

The hug confused me. I hadn't been lying when I'd told Harper that nothing was "going on" between Griffin and me, at least not in a romantic, dramatic Greek god sort of way. But I'd also been wondering if *maybe* he liked me back, just the teeniest, tiniest little bit. Because: the hand-holding? Noticing I was a lefty? Being so interested in norahs? I couldn't help adding it all up and thinking that maybe, possibly, this was a back-and-forth crush situation.

And yet . . . *a hug*? That's what people do when they're trying to cheer you up. You don't hug someone you crush on. You hug people in the hospital, the way the nurses hugged me at Phipps. I had a ton of hug experience these last two years, so I knew what hugs meant. I mean, I didn't know what I wanted from Griffin—but it wasn't a *hug*.

When I got back to Art Club, I thought Harper would

demand a bunch of details. But she didn't even seem interested. She sat hunched over a huge poster board, sketching
away while Astrid was peeking over her shoulder.

"Too abstract," Astrid was telling her. "No one will get it,
Harper."

"No one will get what?" I asked.

Astrid fluttered her smeary purple eyelids at me. "What
she's communicating about Overcoming Challenges. It's for a
mural, so it's all about communicating. And what are *you* doing
here, Norah?"

"I signed up for this club," I announced cheerily. "On
Tuesdays."

"You did? I thought you were doing Bugs."

"I changed my mind."

"Well, you can't do a mural if you're here just once a week."

"Fine with me."

"And it's already incredibly crowded in this studio."

"That's okay. I'm small, so I don't take up much room. Can
I sit here?" I pulled over a chair next to Harper, who sneaked
a smile at me. "Hey, that's a really cool sketch. Can you tell me
what it's about?"

"Sure," Harper exclaimed.

Astrid grunted and stomped off.

"Bugs?" Harper asked, giggling.

I had to laugh too. "Yeah, I know. It was just something I told
her once."

"Anyway, thanks for the save," Harper murmured. "She's driving me bananas."

"I can see why. Just ignore her, Harper."

"Yeah, I wish I could. But she's who decides which murals go up. And I really hope one of them is mine."

I didn't want to say this, but I kind of thought Astrid was right about Harper's sketch. I mean, it didn't communicate anything to me, either. Just shapes: a big round one on a big triangle, and a lot of squiggly bits up and down the sides. Battling cancer was nothing like squiggly bits, or those shapes.

Although if you asked me to draw a picture of what it *was* like, a picture that would "communicate" to everyone who didn't understand, I probably couldn't do a whole lot better.

When Art Club was over, Harper and I waited in the school parking lot for Dad to drive us home. Normally, Harper had to take the late bus home after Art Club, so I was glad we could give her a ride.

We shared a squished granola bar Harper had found at the bottom of her backpack, and watched Aria run circles around the school. Aria was so tall and strong-looking that I couldn't look away. *What must it feel like to be so athletic?* I wondered. Every time she passed us, she gave a little wave, while Harper shouted, "GO, ARIA" and "WOO" and other cheers. The whole time this was happening, Harrison was standing over by the gym doors, watching. I'd never noticed before that he liked Aria, but the way he turned his head every time she zipped by, you could tell he thought she was some kind of superhero. And to be honest, I almost agreed with that opinion.

All of a sudden, I heard a familiar squeal. Thea, dressed in a neon green soccer jersey, was sprinting across the parking lot. Toward Griffin, who was walking by himself as he carried his bass.

As soon as she caught up to him, she threw her arms around him, nearly knocking the bass to the sidewalk. Then she squealed again, and started jumping around like a hot popcorn kernel.

I couldn't watch.

Harper noticed my reaction. "Who's that girl? You know her?"

I shrugged. "Yeah, that's Thea. She's in my math class, and she's friends with Astrid."

"Huh. Well, she really likes that boy, obviously."

I didn't answer.

"Okay," Harper said, searching my face. "So is that *The Boy*?"

"You mean Griffin? Yeah."

Harper shielded her eyes from the sun. "Well, Norah, looks to me like you're in a crush triangle. Although in my opinion *she* likes *him* more than *he* likes *her*."

"Where'd you get that from?"

"She's acting all *animated*. And squealy. But he's basically just standing there."

"That doesn't mean anything," I protested. "He's holding a heavy instrument; he's not going to jump around!"

"Maybe. Although he *could* put it down, you know." She stuffed the granola bar wrapper into her pants pocket. "So what's going on between the two of you, anyway?"

I could see it was a test: Would I shut down again, or would I tell her? But I couldn't think of a reason to avoid the topic of Griffin anymore. And besides, wasn't this what normal friends did in the normal world—talk about crushes?

So I told her everything: about the griffins and the norahs, about the Kraken logo and the hug. She listened without interrupting.

Then she said: "Does he know you're a seventh grader?"

I shook my head.

"And does he know you've been sick?"

"No," I admitted.

"Are you going to tell him?"

"Are you nuts? Why would I?"

"*Why?* So he can see the real you."

"I *am* the real me. And I'm not *lying* to him, Harper."

"Um."

"What does 'um' mean?"

"It means I think you sort of are, actually."

"How can you say that? Just because I'm not going, *Oh hello, Griffin, I think you're nice, what did you write for the third math problem, and by the way, last year I had leukemia—*"

"Well, but it *happened* to you, Norah. It's *important*. Why *not* tell him?"

"Because then he'll feel sorry for me! And we'll have to keep talking about it all the time!"

Harper groaned. "Norah, no one is better than you at not talking. You're like the World Not-Talking *Champion*. So if you don't want to keep discussing it, just tell him that! But not even mentioning it is crazy. And also kind of unfair. To you *and* to him."

Fortunately, that was when Dad's car pulled up. Harper and I got in.

"So sorry, girls," Dad said. "My editor called just as I was running out the door—"

"Not a problem, Mr. Levy," Harper said. "Norah and I love having extra time for girl talk."

The way she said it: "girl *talk*."

CYCLOPS

That evening, I Skyped with Mom ("Norah, you look tired. Are you sure you have enough energy for After-school?"), texted Ayesha (I got a 9/10 on my first two homeworks!), then spent a long time researching kraken. The thing about mythical creatures: No one knows exactly what they looked like, so there are always different versions. In this one article I read, the kraken was described as a giant octopus with spikes on its suckers. Which to me sounded extremely rock band–ish, so I decided to draw it that way.

Around nine thirty, Dad came into my bedroom. "Norah, can we chat a sec? About tomorrow."

"Sure," I said, closing my sketchbook and my laptop.

He sat on my bed. "So this is good news, actually. My editor wants me to cover a player on the triple-A farm team for the

Yankees. They're out in Scranton, Pennsylvania, which means I'll need to spend tomorrow on the road."

My mind raced. "So that means you can't pick me up after school? How will I get home?"

"I thought maybe you could take the school bus home, just for tomorrow. But could we keep that between us?"

"You mean not tell Mom?"

He winced a little. "Well, yeah. Because it *does* violate the No-Bus rule."

A secret from Mom put me on Dad's team, which I didn't appreciate. On the other hand, the No-Bus rule was ridiculous. I mean, I was exposed to school germs *all day*; what could a few extra germs on the school bus do to me? And it was so great how Dad could take a travel assignment again.

"Okay," I said. "Sure."

He smiled. "Terrific. Nicole will stay with you overnight, but she won't get here until dinnertime. Think you can hang out, do homework, fix yourself a snack, until she shows up?"

"Dad, I'm in seventh grade. I'm not a baby!"

"I know." *But you had leukemia, Norah. So that resets the clock.* "Sorry."

"That's okay. And I'm glad you're back to normal. With your job, I mean."

He kissed my cheek. "Me too, sweetheart. Me too."

* * *

Sometimes, when I was in the hospital overnight, I had a sort of nightmare. I say "sort of" because I was awake for it, or at least a version of awake. It usually happened the times I woke up in a dark bed area (we didn't have private rooms) and suddenly I had no idea where I was. Like it felt I wasn't in an actual place, at an actual address on a map; I could have been anywhere, or nowhere. And this was terrifying.

Once I told Ayesha about this not-anywhere feeling. She said she'd had something like it too, when she was a patient. And the way she dealt with it was by telling herself, over and over, that she was somewhere else. It didn't matter where, exactly—just anywhere besides a hospital.

So I tried that too. The next time I woke up in the hospital with that creepy floating-in-space, where-am-I sort of feeling, I played a version of the Room game. I pretended to be a camera in my very own bedroom, noticing every little detail, from left to right. And I can't say it tricked me into believing I wasn't in the hospital, in a sick person's bed, with a hospital bracelet around my wrist—but it did make me feel a little better. And I even dozed off for a bit, eventually.

But that night, after Dad told me about his business trip, I got zero sleep. I tried the Bedroom game, but it didn't work— probably because it was only in the hospital that you felt like you were Nowhere, and needed to convince yourself that you were Somewhere Else. Here in my cozy room with the bright yellow walls and the rainbow-colored quilt on my bed, I had no problem knowing *where* I was: I was home, exactly where I was supposed to be. And the reason I couldn't sleep was that I kept thinking about what Harper had told me: that I was telling Griffin a lie. About *who* I was.

Which was completely wrong of her. And actually, *she* was the one being unfair.

I mean, if he'd asked me what I did last winter break and I'd answered something like *Ah yes, I remember: I went skiing in Vermont*, that would be a lie, because the truth was that I was stuck at the hospital doing all-day chemo, feeling like a blob of oatmeal clogging the drain in the kitchen sink. But he'd never asked a specific question, and I'd never answered anything specifically false. In fact, Griffin and I never discussed facts—we only ever talked about fantasy creatures. So how could you lie if you were talking about fiction? Fiction was nothing but a bunch of lies anyway.

Harper was a great friend, but she didn't understand any of this. And why should she? Yes, she came to the hospital all the time, but *as a visitor*. She wasn't a patient, like me; she never had the scary middle-of-the-night feeling that she'd stopped being part of regular life, that she was floating above it in a kind of endless blank nowhere. So she didn't have anything to forget, or to try to forget. Versus me, who wanted only to go forward. Act normal. *Be* normal.

And anyhow, why should I volunteer personal information to a boy who maybe liked that awful, airy Thea with the squealy laugh?

And only gave me a stupid hug, which meant he felt sorry for me?

The next morning in math, we had a substitute teacher, a rumpled guy who seemed like he'd woken up about fifteen minutes before homeroom. Ms. Perillo had prepared a few worksheets for us, and I guess he was too sleepy to hand them out himself.

So he pointed at me for some reason. "Young man, would you help me distribute these?"

Astrid laughed. Rowan snorted. And Thea did a pouting face at me like *Aww, poor you.*

"My name is Norah," I muttered.

"Sorry, young lady," the sub said, honking his nose into a dirty tissue. "My mistake."

I passed out the worksheets, avoiding eye contact with every single person in the class. Was it possible to be any more humiliated—called "young man" by a teacher who hadn't heard My Whole Story? I felt like a popped balloon.

When I sat down again, there was a folded-up piece of paper on my desk.

I unfolded it.

Green ink. Gel-pen ink.

A drawing. Of what? It looked like a thumb with a giant eye. Underneath it was written: *ICU.*

Intensive Care Unit?

Omigod, is that a hospital reference?

Why would Griffin do that? Does he know about me?

And if he does , does he think this is funny or something?

Barely breathing, I peeked at him.

Griffin ripped off a corner of one of the worksheets, wrote something on it fast, and handed it to me: *Supposed to be Cyclops. Told you I can't draw! Stupid sub is blind. I see you.*

ALL ABOUT FEELINGS

So you were right," Harper said as soon as I sat down next to her in English. "Kylie did get in trouble. Silas, too."

"For what?" I asked her, still distracted by the period before.

"What do you *think*, Norah? Sneaking out to get pizza yesterday. And guess who saw them and told the principal: Ms. Farrell."

This surprised me. Ms. Farrell hadn't struck me as the tattle type. But sneaking out of the building during school hours was pretty serious. "How do you know?"

"Everyone was talking about it in math. They both got a week of detention. So thanks for trying to convince me not to do it."

"You're welcome. Harper?"

"Yeah?"

"Will you come with me to the mall after school today? To get my ears pierced?"

"What?" Harper seemed jolted by my change of subject. "Norah, are you even allowed? I thought you always went straight home."

"Yes, normally, but Dad said I could. He has a business trip, so he can't pick me up today. And I asked my parents if I could pierce my ears after you told me Aria did it at the mall, and they said yes."

All of which was technically true.

"Well, but I have Art Club," Harper began.

I leaned toward her to beg. "*Please? A* sub in math called me 'young man.' That's the second time someone thought I was a boy. And I think earrings will make me feel better. About how I look."

"Oh. Sure. Of course!" Harper was too good a friend to protest that I already looked perfectly wonderful, blahblahblah. And here I was, *actually sharing my feelings* about cancer-ish topics. So of course she was going to be supportive, even if it meant missing Afterschool—and not telling her mom where she went instead.

Class started. Today was especially fun, because Ms. Farrell had us play a game called Greek Gods Couples Counseling, where a god and a goddess who were having relationship issues had to talk to a "therapist." I was in a group with Aria and Harrison; every five minutes we were supposed to switch roles.

First I was Echo and Aria was Narcissus. We argued to Harrison about how we couldn't communicate.

Next Harrison was Orpheus and I was Eurydice, telling Aria about our unfair separation.

Then Aria said: "Okay, I have an idea: Now I'll be Artemis and Harrison will be Actaeon. Norah can be the therapist."

"Wait," Harrison protested. "I don't know that story."

Aria narrowed her eyes. "No problem, Harrison, I'll tell it to you! Artemis is the beautiful goddess of the hunt, right? She's always running after animals in the woods. And one time she stopped to bathe in a little brook. And this hunter guy named Actaeon was in love with her, so he spied on her bathing. But Artemis always needed privacy, so when she realized Actaeon was following her around and spying, she flung some water at him. And when it hit Actaeon's head, antlers grew, and he turned into a stag and ran off."

Harrison squirmed in his chair. "Huh. That's not a very nice story."

"Oh, it's not?" Aria said, her dark eyes flashing. "Which part don't you like, Harrison? Spying on someone when they're trying to run? Or getting punished for it?"

"What?"

"Oh, come on. I *saw* you staring at me yesterday in Afterschool!"

Harrison's eyes rounded. "I wasn't doing anything."

"Don't lie! Of *course* you were watching me. You totally

wrecked my concentration. So all my times were off." Aria raised her eyebrows at me. "Norah was there. I bet she saw you."

"Actually, yeah, " I admitted. "I did notice you yesterday in the parking lot, Harrison." Now he was blushing so hard I thought he might violate the No-Crying rule.

"Sorry," he muttered. "I won't do it again."

"You'd *better* not, at least not without asking me first," Aria warned. "Or I'll turn you into mashed potatoes. With gravy!"

Aria grinned at me. I could see she was just teasing Harrison. But it was cool how she was standing up for herself—jokey about everything except running.

For a second I found myself wishing I could be like Aria Maldonado—or maybe *be* Aria Maldonado. Chatty. Smiley. Athletic. Loud.

"How are we all doing?" Ms. Farrell was at our table, eyeing us. "Resolving conflicts in a peaceful manner befitting deities?"

Aria kept grinning. "Yeah, we are. This is so fun."

"I'm glad you think so. It's a warm-up for our big project." Ms. Farrell winked and walked off.

We played the game for a few more minutes. Then Ms. Farrell wrote two words on the whiteboard:

SYMPATHY

EMPATHY

"Two nice Greek words," Ms. Farrell said. "Along with 'therapist' and 'therapy,' by the way. The Greeks were all about feelings." She pointed to the whiteboard with her blue marker. "So who can tell us what these words mean, and how they're different from each other?"

Harper raised her hand. "Sympathy is when you feel sorry for someone. Empathy is when you feel what someone else is feeling. Like you're putting yourself in their shoes."

"Right." Next to SYMPATHY, Ms. Farrell wrote FEELING FOR. Next to EMPATHY, she wrote FEELING WITH. "Which is harder—sympathy or empathy?"

"Sympathy," Addison guessed. "Because you see why things are hard for someone else, but you can't always help them."

Ms. Farrell looked at me. "Norah? What do you think?"

I swallowed. "I wasn't raising my hand."

"Yes. But I thought you might have an insight to share."

"Why?"

It sounded like back talk, but I didn't care. She was putting me on the spot, making me talk about cancer. Not directly, but I could tell what she was doing. Like: *Hey, guys, don't feel sorry FOR me; try to feel WITH me.* As if that was possible.

Everyone was staring at me now.

"Just answer," Harper muttered. "Don't do this."

Fine. I took a breath. "I think empathy is harder because when you put yourself in someone else's shoes, sometimes you feel things you don't want to. But I don't think empathy is always possible, anyhow."

"How come?" Ms. Farrell asked, tucking some loose hair behind her ears.

"Because sometimes the other person's experience is so weird that you *can't* put yourself in their shoes. I mean, you may *think* you can, but you really can't."

"I don't agree," Addison called out. "People aren't stupid, Norah."

"I'm not calling anyone stupid," I said.

"Omigod, you so are! You're saying people can't understand some things, even if they want to. And to be honest, I think that's a pretty stuck-up attitude."

"That's not what Norah said," Harper protested. "She said that sometimes it's hard to empathize. *Sometimes.*"

"All right, girls," Ms. Farrell said calmly. "Let's stay on topic here, please. So let me ask you: In the Couples Counseling game, which were you feeling for your characters—sympathy or empathy?"

"Sympathy," Addison said. "Because when I was playing Hera, I felt sorry for her. Zeus was a terrible husband, but she couldn't divorce him, right? So there was no way to help her." Addison shook her braids.

"For me it was empathy," Aria said. "Because I felt *exactly* the same as Artemis when she got spied on." She raised her eyebrows at Harrison, who seemed to shrink.

Ms. Farrell nodded. "Okay, well, for this first project of the year, I'm asking you all to use your strongest *empathic* powers. You're going to pick a mythic character—a god or goddess, a mortal affected by the gods, a creature, any character in any one of the myths—and put yourself in his or her shoes."

"Did the gods wear shoes?" Harrison asked.

"I'm pretty sure they wore sandals," Kylie said. "You know, with those tie-up laces."

"*Figurative* shoes," Ms. Farrell corrected herself. "And you'll prepare a five-minute speech from that character's point of view. Feel what the character is feeling; express his or her thoughts in the first person. Help us to understand your character's behavior, even if it's hard. *Especially* if it's hard. And be creative. Wear costumes, use props. Yes, Malik?"

"Can we have special effects? Like if we pick Zeus, can we have a thunderbolt?"

"Malik, you're not going to electrocute anyone, right?" Kylie asked, giggling.

Ms. Farrell held up a hand. "Guys, I want you to have fun with this project, and be theatrical—but the focus should be on your *words*. And I should tell you that the three best speeches from this class will be delivered to a special school assembly promoting empathy."

"What if you'd rather not?" Cait asked in a small voice.

"No one will be forced onstage, Cait. But you do need to do your speech for this class, okay?"

"Okay," Cait said, melting into her seat.

"What if you can't pick *anyone*?" Addison asked.

"If you're having trouble coming up with a character, I'll try to help you find a good fit. Or you can ask our expert mythologist,

Norah, if she has any suggestions." Ms. Farrell smiled at me, but I didn't smile back.

And then Stinkeye Number Three happened. I tried to ignore Addison, but she refused to look away.

The bell rang.

"Let me know if there are more questions," Ms. Farrell called as we got up to leave the room. "And I want to hear which character you've chosen by Friday!"

A PAIR OF GREEN DRAGONS

The rest of the day zoomed by. When Harper told Aria our plan for the afternoon, Aria surprised me by offering to come with us. I'd never been to Mimi's, the place where Aria had had her ears done, and I was pretty sure we could get there by bus—but Aria said her mom would drive us. In fact, her mom would come inside the store with us; for piercing, they made you have a grown-up with you, Aria said.

At dismissal, Aria's mom was already waiting in the parking lot.

"This is such a fabulous idea," Mrs. Maldonado gushed. "Norah, you'll look so pretty with earrings!"

"I don't need to look pretty," I admitted. "I just don't want to be called 'young man' anymore."

"If anyone calls you that, just tell me, Norah, and I'll turn them into mashed potatoes," Aria shouted. "With gravy! What kind of earrings do you want?"

"Big fat dangly ones."

"You know, they start you off with tiny studs," Harper said. "You have to wear them for a month."

"An entire *month*?" By then, my hair would be almost long enough. Almost.

Aria grinned at me. "Yeah, but once the month is over, you can wear whatever you like. I plan to get giant hoops with perches for birds. Or lightsabers. Or light-up Christmas trees."

"You're going to get regular earrings that won't pull your earlobes off," Mrs. Maldonado said, pretending not to smile. "And Norah, I do have to ask: Your parents are both okay with this? Because I'm a little nervous that we haven't spoken directly—"

"Oh, don't worry, they totally are!" I swore. "Anyhow, Mom's back in California and Dad's out of town right now, so thanks for taking me."

"You're very welcome, dear. I'm just happy to do this."

When we got to the mall, Harper said she needed a snack, so first we went to get cinnamon pretzels. The pretzels made us thirsty, so we got shakes. (Mine was strawberry/banana/mango; it was so delicious I finished the whole thing without realizing it.) Then Aria asked if we could possibly buy some lip gloss "really fast." I said sure—not only because it felt so great just wandering aimlessly around a shopping mall, but also because Aria-without-Kylie was a loud, fun person who knew song lyrics. Also, her mom didn't helicopter; she kept popping into shoe stores, so it almost felt like the three of us were on our own, singing, staring at shop windows, eating junk food.

Seriously, it was the most fun I'd had in eons.

At four, we all went to Mimi's, a store where the music was Japanese and the signs were pink and lowercase. A young woman who reminded me of Ayesha—dark skin, long black hair in a tight, high ponytail, a million studs in each ear—announced in a bored voice that to get my ears pierced I needed to have a parent present.

"And here I am," Mrs. Maldonado announced in a don't-mess-with-me voice. "A present parent."

I thought Almost Ayesha would make Mrs. Maldonado show some ID to prove she was *my* parent. Because, I mean, she didn't look *anything* like me—her skin was light brown, and she was very tall, like Aria. But Almost Ayesha just checked her watch, yawned, handed me an "ear care pamphlet," and led me over to a pink-curtained booth labeled **ear's lookin' at you, kid!** I meant to ask how they were sterilizing the ear-piercer thing— but before I knew it, she'd punched two holes in my earlobes, and stuck in tiny silver balls.

Harper handed me a mirror. "Norah, I love it! You look incredible!"

"Woo, Norah!" Aria did a dance move that was mostly elbows.

BARBARA DEE

"Mom, can we pleeeease get these for me?" She grabbed a pair of earrings that looked like thunderbolts, and held them up to her ears. When they jiggled, they lit up and made a zapping noise. "MUST HAVE THESE FOR MY GOD COSTUME."

I had to laugh. "You're doing Zeus?"

"I might!" Aria answered, still dancing. "He'd totally rock thunderbolt earrings!"

"Ooh, guys," Harper exclaimed as she peered into a glass case. "Norah, see those earrings that look like paintbrushes? They're so cute, aren't they?"

"Yeah," I agreed. "But I really love these." I pointed to a pair of green dragons breathing orange fire. They had red beads for eyes and purple beads on their tails, like scales.

"Mom?" Aria begged. "Momomom?"

Mrs. Maldonado sighed. After twelve years, you could tell she was used to Aria. "All right. You can have the thunderbolts, as long as you wait the full month to wear them."

"Aww, Mom. Come on, I *promise* I won't get an infection!"

"I mean it, Aria. One month of antibiotic ointment and studs, or no deal." She glanced at Almost Ayesha, who didn't take her eyes off her phone as she gave a thumbs-up.

And I thought: This is what it's like for Aria. A trip to the mall, a jokey argument with your mom about ointment and earrings. Nothing life-or-death. Traffic and weather on the eights.

Then I noticed Mrs. Maldonado pointing to the dragon earrings. Almost Ayesha asked if she wanted to add them to the cost of the ear piercing. Mrs. Maldonado said yes, taking out her credit card and handing it to Almost Ayesha.

Suddenly I understood what was happening. Mrs. Maldonado was paying for the whole thing—the ear piercing, the silver studs, plus the dragon earrings—making them a gift to me. A cancer consolation prize.

"Wait, no," I sputtered. "Thanks, Mrs. Maldonado, but you really don't have to—"

She pressed her hand on my shoulder. "But I want to, honey. I insist."

Was that empathy or sympathy? Maybe it was something else—relief that her own daughter was healthy—that had nothing to do with me. Whatever it was, I had a squirmy feeling in my stomach that wasn't from cinnamon pretzels and the strawberry/banana/mango shake. And now this outing, which had been so fun, was just turning into a whole cancer thing.

It was SO UNFAIR. I could feel hot tears start to prick my eyes, so I blinked fast.

But I think Mrs. Maldonado noticed, because she tugged me away from Aria and Harper, who were laughing hysterically at some nose studs.

"Norah," she said quietly. "This has nothing to do with your being sick. It's just regular girl stuff, you know? I was glad to do it for Aria, and now I'm glad to do it for you. Okay?"

"Okay," I said, feeling my face relax into a smile.

BARBARA DEE

Because: "regular girl stuff"?

Those were like the three happiest words ever.

When I got home, Nicole was in the kitchen. This time, instead of greeting me with a hug and chicken potpie, she yelled. "Norah, where *were* you?"

"At the mall with my friends." I stared at her, shocked by the yelling. Also by the fact that she was there. "Dad said you'd be coming at suppertime."

"I left work early. To be here for you!"

"Oh. You didn't have to do that."

"No, I realize that, but I *wanted* to. You were supposed to come straight home. What were you doing at the mall?"

Probably it was stupid of me, but I'd always thought Nicole and I were friends. I mean, she'd never acted all parent-y; she even called me "girl" sometimes. So I thought if I showed her my earlobes, she'd understand how I felt about the "young man" stuff. She'd *empathize*.

I pointed to my ears. With my Regular Girl Stuff silver studs.

"What?" Nicole demanded. "What are you showing me?" The earrings must have caught the light or something, because suddenly she understood. "Oh! Norah, you *didn't*. No way!"

"What's wrong?" I asked.

"What's *wrong*? Norah, you went out and got your *ears* pierced? Without your parents' permission?"

"No, no. I had their permission! Mom even said she'd take me!"

"When she was here, in New York, which she obviously isn't! Does she even know about this?"

Now I was getting angry. Since when had Nicole taken Mom's side against me? And why was she yelling?

"Something happened in school today that meant I *couldn't* wait for Mom," I said. "And I'll explain that *to her*."

"Go ahead!" Nicole crossed her arms like: *I dare you.*

"I will. I was going to Skype with her later, anyway."

"No, Norah. I want you to call her *now*. And I want to listen in."

"Are you serious?" I squealed. "Anyhow, there's a time difference with California. And she could be teaching."

"If it's inconvenient, she won't pick up. Just call her!"

"Nicole, back off," I said, my voice shaking with anger. "This has nothing to do with you, okay? You're not even *in* my family, so truthfully, what I do with my earlobes isn't any of your business!"

"If that's how you feel about me, fine," she snapped. "Nice to know."

I went to my room and slammed the door.

HERA

I didn't call Mom right away, because first I wanted to calm down. For about an hour I plopped on my bed and drew krakens—swirly, spiky, tentacled creatures with suction cups and angry eyes. I also drew my new dragon earrings—not as earrings, but as twin creatures I named Flame and Sizzle. Although those names kind of sounded like a hamburger restaurant (The Flame 'n' Sizzle), so I changed my mind.

Then I read *D'Aulaires' Book of Greek Myths*. I told myself I was doing homework, deciding on my god for the English project—even though it never occurred to me to pick anyone besides Persephone. Because not only did I love that story, but also the whole thing about the daughter being separated from her mother kind of applied to me, in a way. I mean, it wouldn't be super-hard to empathize with Persephone.

At nine p.m. (my time), I called Mom. As soon as I saw her

nonsmiling face on my laptop, I knew she'd already heard about my ears.

"Dad texted me," she said. "Nicole called him with the news. Why couldn't you wait for me, like we agreed?"

I told her about the stupid sub. And then, because without knowing the rest, the stupid sub's mistake wouldn't seem important, I told her about Griffin. Not that I had a crush on him, not the kraken stuff, just that he was sort of a friend whose opinion I cared about. But I think she understood anyway.

Also, I told her how Astrid had laughed at me. And how Thea was all *Poor you*.

"Norah, you can't let other people rule your life," Mom said. "If that sub was too sleepy to get a good look at you, who cares *what* he thinks. And those girls sound nasty, anyway."

"I know, but—"

"Are you going to punch holes in your ears every time someone says a stupid or mean thing? Because your ears are going to be Swiss cheese."

It was such a ridiculous image that we both had to laugh.

Then Mom said she was mad at Aria's mom for not checking with her about the earring thing. I begged her not to say anything to Mrs. Maldonado, who was only trying to be nice by doing Regular Girl Stuff. And I showed Mom my silver balls and also the green dragons, which she admitted were incredibly cool.

"All right," she finally said, exhaling. "So here's what I have to say about all this: I'm upset that you didn't wait for me, Norah.

BARBARA DEE

But I'm much *more* upset that you did it behind our backs, when you'd promised Dad and me that we could trust you."

I chewed on my lip. "Sorry."

"Because seriously, honey, do I have to spell this out for you? If your friends do something dumb, if they get their ears pierced somewhere unsanitary, they get an infection. Big deal. But you're in a *completely different category*, you know? You can't just . . ." She shook her head helplessly.

I knew what she wanted to say: *You can't just make normal growing-up mistakes. Because nothing will ever be normal for you. Or for any of us. Not completely.*

Because you're not a Regular Girl.

"Mom, it was completely sanitary," I said in a shaky voice.

"I certainly hope so."

"And I won't do anything like that ever again, I *swear*."

"Good. Don't. One more thing. I'm very upset with how you treated Nicole."

"What?"

"You heard me. You told her she wasn't in our family. But she is, and I need you to apologize to her immediately."

I couldn't believe this. Mom and Nicole were supposed to hate each other. Or, if not hate, then at least resent. I mean, *D'Aulaires'* was full of stories about how Hera treated Zeus's girlfriends. Like how when Hera found out Leto was pregnant, she ordered every country on earth to banish her. And how she tricked Semele into asking Zeus to reveal himself, causing

Semele to burn to cinders. And how she punished Echo by taking away her ability to speak her own words.

Hera was badass. Scary. But she was Zeus's wife, so you could understand her jealousy. Empathize with it, almost.

Versus Mom sticking up for Dad's girlfriend, which made *zero sense*.

But I promised to apologize to Nicole anyway. The truth was, my stomach was still feeling sort of squirmy—and at least part of that had to be from guilt. Nicole was a good person, and she didn't deserve how I'd treated her.

As soon as I logged off Skype, I went into the living room, where Nicole was watching the movie *Alien*. I sat on the sofa about a foot away from her, but she held out one arm for me to snuggle next to her. So I did, even though every time that movie was on, I switched the channel.

"Nice ears," she said, not taking her eyes off the TV. "It'll be fun to get new earrings once your holes are all healed. Are you hungry?"

"Not really. My stomach is feeling weird from all the junk I ate at the mall."

"Well, junk food with friends is important. Once in a while, anyway . . . as long as it's not behind your parents' backs."

"I know. I should have told them about the mall. And the earrings. And sorry I said that stuff to you before—"

"Shh, girl," Nicole said. "This scene is gross, and I want to watch."

The next morning I woke up feeling I'd been trampled on by a giant centaur. When Nicole called me downstairs to breakfast, I could barely move. Everything ached—even my fingers. Also, everything felt fuzzy, a million miles away. And when Nicole presented me with what she'd cooked—puffy French toast with cinnamon butter and sliced apples—I just stared at my plate, trying to remember what was so great about food.

"You don't like it? I could make you something else," she said, already opening the fridge door.

"No, it looks delicious. I'm just not super-hungry this morning. I think that shake I had at the mall upset my stomach or something."

Nicole frowned at me. "Still? You said your stomach felt weird last night. Maybe you should stay home from school."

"No!" I nearly shouted that at her, so I cleared my throat, as if: *throat malfunction*. "No, I can't. We have a math test today, and I need to tell my English teacher which god I'm choosing for this project—"

"Listen, Norah, everything is secondary to your health."

"My health is great." I took a giant forkful of French toast to prove it. "Hey, this is yum. Thanks for making it, Nicole."

She narrowed her eyes as if she could tell I was full of it. So I had to keep eating, even though my stomach protested *Nooo, stooop*.

I wasn't lying, at least not about the math test. As soon as I saw Griffin right before first period, I could tell he was nervous about it, so I tried to cheer him up.

"I've been sketching krakens," I told him. "They look really cool. Want to see?"

His eyes lit up. "Yeah, I do. But first I should look over my notes, okay?"

"Oh, of course."

"Can you show me at lunch?"

"Today?"

He nodded. Because of course he meant today.

"Sure," I said, thinking: *Eep. Now I'll have to skip health class. After just promising Mom that she could trust me.*

Here we go again.

EVIL BUG

Except that day I never made it to lunch. Or health.

I barely made it through math. Barely finished the test.

As soon as I got to English, I told Ms. Farrell I needed to go to the nurse's office. "Oh, of course," she said with worried eyes. She told Harper to walk with me, "just for company." And I felt so awful I didn't even protest.

Mrs. Donaldson looked me over, felt my forehead, and led me to Norah's Cot. "Lie down," she said softly. "I'm calling your mom."

"You can't. She's in California."

"Okay, your Dad, then."

"He's out of town. At a baseball game."

She stared at me like *Are your parents INSANE?* So I explained about Dad's work, and how Nicole was staying with me overnight. Mrs. Donaldson asked for Nicole's phone number, and for a minute I was a total blank. Then I remembered it was programmed into my phone, which I just handed to her.

She called Nicole. I was feeling so woozy I can't remember what happened, how long I was asleep, or how much time things took. But the next thing I remember, Nicole was sitting on the edge of the cot in her black going-to-work pantsuit, looking at me with a weird expression.

"So I guess you really hated that French toast, huh?" she said when she saw I was awake.

"No, no, it wasn't that—"

"Come on, silly, I was joking. Let's get you home now, okay?"

Harper brought my stuff from my locker, and somehow I made it to Nicole's car.

The next few days were a blur.

I was sick. Not cancer-sick, germ-sick. The evil bug that had attacked me was from school, or the mall, or Aria's car, or the hospital. Or possibly it was from my house, even my own bedroom. There was no way to know. And no way to stop more germ attacks from beating me, as long as my immune system was still "compromised."

This is what Dr. Choi said when Dad took me to Phipps.

"As long as Norah's out in the world, it'll be a constant battle," she told Dad, even though I was sitting right there on the examining table. Dr. Glickstein never talked about me as if I weren't there, but he was busy seeing some kid who was "having an emergency," Dr. Choi explained. So I was being seen by a doctor who'd never even met me before this very minute, and didn't know the first thing about my personality.

"Is Norah getting enough rest?" she asked Dad.

"YES, I AM," I answered.

"Because that's the most important thing. If she's run-down, she's much more vulnerable to whatever virus is going around the school."

"I KNOW."

"Would she agree to wearing a surgical mask in the halls?"

"Wait," I exploded. "You're asking Dad if *I* would wear a mask? Every time *I* switched classes? You should ask *me*."

Dr. Choi blinked. "I beg your pardon, Norah. A surgical mask is one solution, yes. Another would be leaving class five minutes early, just to reduce the number of germs you're in contact with in the hallway every time the bell rings."

Dad glanced at me, nodding. "All right, thanks, Dr. Choi. We'll discuss it."

On the ride home, I informed Dad that I absolutely refused to wear a mask. Not a surgical mask, not a Halloween mask, not a hockey mask. No mask, period. As for the five-minute thing, maybe. *Maybe.* I'd think about it.

Dad sighed. "Norah, it's not really up to you."

"Who's it up to, then?"

"No comment."

"You? Mom? But *it's my body*! And I'm sick of people talking *about* it as I'm not even there!"

Before he could say anything to defend Dr. Choi, I added: "I *hate* this, Dad. Why can't I just go to school and have a regular, boring, normal life like everyone else?"

Dad reached over and rubbed my arm. "Because the evil Luke Emia still has his eye on you, baby. And he's mad that you've been giving him the slip."

I stayed home from school the rest of that week, and the whole week after that. Mom flew home for the weekend, just to make sure I didn't need to be in the hospital, she said—even though Dr. Choi said I should rest at home. The whole time Mom was here, she kept unbunching towels and Lysoling everything, almost as if she was accusing Dad of making me sick with his germy surfaces. And the funny thing was how Nicole didn't stay away for Mom's sake. It was like they'd come to some kind of agreement—about me, apparently.

In the middle of the second week, Harper came over after school to give me notes.

"Aren't you missing Afterschool?" I asked her.

Harper shrugged. "Yeah, but I'm happy to get a day off from Astrid." She described how she'd put up her mural—carefully, over four afternoons—only for Astrid to insist she take the whole thing down.

"Why?"

"Same old criticism. It doesn't 'communicate.' I feel like communicating with *her*."

"So why don't you?"

"Because what good would it do? She's still in charge. She's still horrible. Oh, and by the way, I saw your boyfriend."

"What?" My heart bounced like a Super Ball. "You mean Griffin?"

"Yep. Astrid told him we were friends in Art Club or something, so he gave me this for you." From her backpack she pulled out a folded-up piece of paper, all taped shut. A note mummy.

She waited for me to open it. When she saw I wasn't going to, at least not in front of her, she smiled. "Also, Ms. Castro wants to know if you need anything, and Ms. Farrell says hi. Aria and Cait say get better soon. And Silas wants to know when you're coming back."

"Really? What does *he* care?"

"He said he wants to talk to you."

"About what?"

"You're asking *me*?" She tapped on my friendship bracelet, the one she'd given me when I first went into the hospital. "Hey, you're still wearing it."

"Of course. I never take it off. You're my best friend, Harper."

"And you're mine." She threw her arms around me, and I didn't even care that she was full of germs. Because they were best-friend germs, the kind that make you feel better.

"Sorry I've been so weird about things," I said into her hair.

"That's okay," Harper replied. "You have the right to be weird. For a few more weeks, anyway."

"A few more *weeks*? What if I'm not finished by then?"

"Joking. Take all the time you need." She pulled away, smiling. "But really, Norah, come back to school soon. Stuff keeps happening and you should be there with me, okay?"

"Okay," I said, smiling back at her.

As soon as Harper left, I untaped Griffin's message. He'd drawn a messy octopus next to a bad cyclops. Underneath, written in green gel pen, it said:

    👁 *MISS U.*

    ♡, *GRIFFIN*

PINK

Mom said she refused to let me go back to school the next Monday without looking me over in person, so she flew back to New York for the second straight weekend. I argued that it was completely unnecessary and a waste of money, but she insisted. Anyway, I told myself, Demeter would have done the same thing for Persephone, and there was no point arguing with a fierce Greek goddess.

As soon as she walked into the house, she gave her expert diagnosis. "Norah, you still look *a bit iffy*. Greg, doesn't Norah look *iffy* to you?"

"Well . . . ," Dad began.

"Maybe if you rested at home just a few more days—"

"NO," I answered. By then I was demented with boredom, and why couldn't Persephone could be just as fierce as Demeter? "That's impossible, Mom! If I'm tired at school, I'll just rest on my cot. But I'm going back on Monday. I *have* to."

Mom looked at Dad, who shrugged like *I give up*. Then Nicole brought me a mug of tea, basically announcing that now there were *three* grown-ups paying attention to me, so I'd better not try anything funny, young lady.

And the four of us had a really nice weekend, actually. All three grown-ups took me apple picking on Saturday, and for dinner we went out for spicy ramen. On Sunday, Mom took me to the mall—for snow boots, she said, although we ended up buying origami earrings shaped like octopii.

On Sunday night, Mom told me she'd arranged her schedule to stay in New York a few more days. She said her students had "study days"—but I knew she was sticking around to make sure I was okay. And this time I didn't argue.

On Monday morning, I was so excited I could barely eat breakfast. I dressed extra carefully, putting on a pretty blue top and a black skirt that Nicole had ordered for me online. When Dad told me we needed to leave ten minutes earlier than usual because he needed to meet with his editor, I was glad. I'd never told Ms. Farrell I'd chosen Persephone for the speech project, and I wanted to talk to her about it before homeroom.

When I entered the school building, there was Malik, putting up more MALIK FOR PREZ posters in front of the main office. He waved at me casually, as if I'd been in school just yesterday. I waved back. *Poor Malik*, I thought. *He's taking it so seriously. Why don't people care about this election as much as he does?*

Then I heard someone shouting my name.

"Norah! Norah Levy! Over here!"

The shout was coming from down the hallway, which was lined with tables. I started walking over, and immediately saw that the tables were crammed with baked stuff—cookies, muffins, brownies, slices of cake. A lot of pink frosting. Pink sprinkles.

"Hey, Norah, wanna buy a cookie to end breast cancer?" Thea was yelling at me, waving her arms. "We have chocolate chip, oatmeal raisin, shortbread, gingerbread—"

I stopped in front of her. She had a giant pink ribbon pinned to her hoodie, and a pink baseball cap that said 8TH GRADE BAKE SALE in sequins. Which were also pink.

"Everything's a dollar," Thea announced. Lifting her chin to look past me at the kids streaming into the building, she launched into her spiel: "We're raising money to fight breast cancer, which affects two hundred fifty thousand women in America every year. That's one in eight women in this country alone. So you should *definitely* support our bake sale, because it's for *a very important cause.*"

Now my eyes focused on the posters behind her, all of them either on pink oaktag or written in giant pink letters:

SUPPORT THE EIGHTH GRADE BAKE SALE TO END BREAST CANCER!

COOKIES FOR CANCER AWARENESS!
AARON BURR EIGHTH GRADE FOR THE CURE!
BE SWEET! BUY SWEET! BATTLE CANCER!

I stood there, staring.

Astrid came over. She was entirely pinked out: pink hair with a giant pink ribbon, pink eye shadow, pink sweatshirt, pink fuzzy slippers.

"Hey, Nor-*ahh*," she said in a singsongy voice. "Come on, buy a cookie! Don't you want to help us end breast cancer?"

"Are you serious?" I blurted.

She laughed. "Don't we *look* serious?"

"Actually, no." My heart was banging. "I think you look ridiculous."

"Excuse me?"

"In all that pink. Like if you wear pink, that means you're anti-breast cancer. Because, you know, breast cancer is *terrified* of the color pink."

Kids were crowding the tables now. Some of them were grabbing cookies, but many were just spectating, watching a fight that was starting to get good. I was recognizing faces in the crush of kids: Malik. Kylie. Harrison. Cait. Addison. But I didn't care. I was so mad right then, I was almost vibrating.

"Norah, that's not what this is about, okay?" Thea said in her airiest voice. "You're totally missing the point."

"No, Thea, I totally get it. You think if you sell a few oat-meal raisin cookies and Astrid dresses like a bottle of Pepto-

Bismol, you get to feel all proud of yourselves, right?"

Astrid's mouth dropped open. Even her tongue was pink. "Norah, omigod, *what* is your *problem*? Breast cancer is a terrible disease! How can you *possibly* not support our fight against it?"

"I do support it! I'm just against people who don't know anything *about* cancer acting like they own it, like it's their cute little pet cause!"

"Who's that girl?" someone was asking. "Why is she saying that?"

Good question, I thought. *Why was I making a scene?*

I should just shut up.

I should leave.

Or maybe the floor could crack open and swallow me, like Persephone.

But it didn't. Instead, I watched, barely breathing, as Malik bought himself a muffin with pink sprinkles on top. Then as Kylie helped herself to a pink ribbon, which she pinned to her sweater.

Kylie. The person who wouldn't let me talk about cancer, because it was "too depressing." Who was now decorating herself with a ribbon, like she was some kind of war hero. It felt like everything about me was being deleted.

And that was when I realized I didn't care. About how much I said. Or didn't say. What people thought about me. What they felt.

"You know what, Astrid?" I could hear myself shouting, which was totally unnecessary, because Astrid was right in front of me. "You keep saying 'fight cancer,' but you don't have a clue what that means. It has *nothing* to do with cookies or posters. Or stupid pink frosting!"

"Omigod, this is insane," Astrid said. She flipped her pink hair. "Look, Norah, you don't need to be like this. We *know* you were sick, okay? We totally get it."

"What?" My heart stopped. "You *know*? About my—"

"Yes, we heard. And we're very sorry, all right? But this bake sale isn't *about* you."

That did it. "Don't you *dare*," I hissed. "Don't you *dare* say it's not about me! *You* don't get to decide—"

"Norah."

I hadn't seen her in the crowd, but all of a sudden Harper was grabbing my sleeve. "Come on, okay? Let's get out of here."

"NO!" I yanked my arm from her. It was like I was on fire, and I wasn't done burning. "You know what else, Astrid? People fight all different kinds of cancer, not just breast cancer, and not even just mine. And no one dresses up for them and bakes brownies. But they deserve it just as much, okay? So if you enjoy feeling sorry for sick people, if it makes you feel superior and noble, think about *them*! Or anyone besides yourself! And you too, Thea! And Kylie—"

"Norah?"

I whipped my head around. Griffin was standing right next

to me. His face was pale and his big brown eyes were huge. Full of questions.

"Norah?" he repeated. "What's going on?"

I opened my mouth to explain, but I couldn't talk. Couldn't breathe.

So I ran.

CAPTIVITY

"Norah? Come on, we see your feet, we can tell you're in there."

Harper was in front of my bathroom stall, but I didn't answer. I couldn't.

"You're going to lock yourself in the toilet all day? Are you all right?"

Obviously not. If you're all right, you don't lock yourself in the toilet, do you?

"Can I do anything? Do you need anything?"

How about an escape ladder? Or a catapult?

"Norah, it's Aria," Aria said. "I'm here too."

Oh, great. Let's all eat cinnamon pretzels.

"Norah, what happened?" Harper asked. "Why were you so mad at them?"

"Don't you want to raise money, even *if* those cookies looked gross?" Aria asked.

I didn't answer. Because I couldn't. The shock that Thea and Astrid—and maybe Griffin, too—had known about me all along, the sick feeling that I'd totally lost it in front of everyone—it was too much. Too much to have to think of words.

"We should go get someone," Harper murmured. "I'm worried."

"Who's her guidance counselor?" Aria asked.

"Ms. Castro."

"Don't get Ms. Castro," I blurted.

"Norah?" Harper pressed against the door. "Hey. You okay?"

"No. But don't get Ms. Castro."

"Promise. Will you come out, then?"

"No."

"But it's stinky in here."

That's my problem, not yours. Just leave if you don't like it.

Pause. Now they were whispering.

"Well, fine, Norah," Aria announced. "But if you refuse to open the door, we're definitely getting *someone*. So just tell us who you want it to be."

"Ms. Farrell." I didn't know where that answer came from, but it's what I said.

Aria ran out of the girls' room. So now it was just Harper and me. I could tell she'd sat herself in front of my stall, guarding it like she was Cerberus, the three-headed watchdog of the underworld. Although I had no idea what she was guarding it from. Ms. Castro, maybe. Or Astrid and Thea.

"Aria was right: Those cookies looked gross," she said. "You can tell they bought cookie dough."

Who cares about the stupid cookie dough. Do you think that's the issue?

"Astrid's so horrible. It was cool how you told her off. I wish I could do that."

You can, Harper. It's easy. Just open your mouth.

She kept chatting, but I didn't listen. Something about Art Club. Overcoming Challenges. Whatever. I could tell she was trying her best to distract me, even though she was freaked about my behavior—so part of me kept thinking how lucky I was to have such a good friend. But another part of me kept wishing she would just shut up, let me hide by myself in peace.

The girls' room door creaked. Aria and Ms. Farrell burst in.

"Norah, you okay?" Ms. Farrell asked. She sounded worried.

"I want to go home," I blurted. It wasn't until I said this that I knew it was what I wanted. I wanted it as much as I ever had in my whole life—even when I was Nowhere in the hospital, in the middle of the night.

"Absolutely," Ms. Farrell said. "Would you like to go to the nurse's office while we contact your parents?"

"No."

"Really? Because I'm sure you'd be more comfortable on your cot—"

"No thank you."

"All right, sweetheart." It sounded weird; teachers didn't call you names like that after preschool. But because it was Ms. Farrell, I didn't mind.

"Your mom is in California?" she asked.

She's done her homework. "Yes, but she's still here for a few days. In New York."

"Great. I'm going to go call her now. Harper and Aria will stay here with you."

"You don't have to. I can call her."

"Yes, but I'd prefer to contact her myself, if that's okay."

Not waiting for my answer, Ms. Farrell left the bathroom.

Nobody said anything for a while. Then Aria started singing. She did some dance moves which I couldn't see, but I could tell they involved elbows, because it was that sort of music. Anyway, it took my mind off the bathroom stinkiness.

About five minutes later, Ms. Farrell returned. Mom was on her way, she said.

By then I was feeling stiff and crampy. But I refused to leave the stall. I wouldn't come out until Mom had rescued me from this place, and I knew I'd never have to return here, ever.

Ever, ever, ever.

Q AND A

om didn't ask any questions or even say very much the whole ride home. It wasn't until we were in the living room and she'd made us both some chai that she asked me what had happened. So I told her.

She tucked her legs underneath her in a cozy way, like it was her sofa and she still lived here. "These were the eighth grade girls you'd mentioned before? From your math class?"

I nodded.

"Okay," Mom said. "So can you explain why you reacted— why their bake sale affected you so much, honey? Because isn't it a *good* thing to try to cure breast cancer?"

"Sure," I said limply. "Of course."

"And, you know, not so long ago, people didn't talk about breast cancer. Or any cancer, really. So it's great that breast cancer is out in the open now, and so many women are embracing it as a cause, raising awareness, doing walkathons—"

"Mom, I *know*. It wasn't *about* breast cancer."

"Well, what was it about, then? I feel like I'm missing something."

But so was I. It was weird how I couldn't explain my meltdown, especially about something like a fund-raiser to end *cancer*, of all things. Sure, Thea and Astrid were acting smug and clueless and obnoxious—but why should their dumb behavior have set me off like that? And now I'd humiliated myself in front of everyone. Especially Griffin. WHY?

All I knew for sure was that school was over for me. I'd tried to return, it was a worthwhile experiment, but the whole thing was hopeless. I couldn't pretend I'd never been sick, because that's who I was, The Girl Who; but I couldn't explain what that meant, because to do it I'd have to speak Martian. So it was like I was trapped halfway between two worlds—Sick and Not-Sick— and didn't completely belong in either one.

Mom sipped her tea. "You know, sweetheart, a few days ago you wouldn't even consider staying home to rest. You said you *had* to go back to school. Remember?"

"Yes, but I was wrong," I said quickly. "Can't I just work with Ayesha from now on? *Please?*"

She put down her mug. "You mean not go to school anymore?"

I nodded.

"Norah—" Mom began.

"You saw how great I did with her! She got me so far ahead I'm not even in seventh grade math and science! If I worked with her now that I actually have energy, I'd get even further ahead!"

"Maybe you would. But it's not a race."

"Will you even consider it?"

She sighed. "I'll discuss it with your dad."

"That means no."

"Norah—"

"You always *say* you're going to discuss things, but you never do!"

"That isn't true, honey. We just discuss things on our own timetable."

"Which is always too slow!"

Mom kissed my cheek and went off to make some phone calls. I could tell she was calling California. It occurred to me that maybe she was working out a way not to go back to the university—and really, if I was quitting Burr to homeschool, it would probably affect her job. Especially if Dad was traveling for his magazine again.

But I couldn't worry about that now.

I drank my tea and thought about Ayesha.

When Dad came home that evening, I expected to have the same conversation all over again. *Q: Why did you react so strongly to the stupid bake sale? A: I don't know!* But he didn't even mention it. He just asked me if I wanted chicken or spaghetti for supper, and then afterward suggested we watch a movie. I guess maybe he thought it would all blow over, and tomorrow morning he'd be driving me to school, just like normal.

I woke at the regular time. I didn't want him to think I was being lazy. It wasn't about lazy.

"Norah, you took the check I wrote for lunch money?" he asked, not looking up from his phone as he sipped his coffee.

"Dad, please listen. I'm really, really not going back there," I said, as calmly as I could. "Didn't Mom tell you? I just want to homeschool with Ayesha."

He rubbed his chin, which he hadn't shaved yet. "Do you really mean this?"

"Yep. And you know how stubborn I can be. So will you *please, please* call her?"

"All right. But no promises. Your mom and I—"

"I know. We're on different speeds. I'll try to be patient."

"Thank you. Much appreciated."

"But I'm not promising I'll *stay* patient."

ROCK STAR

The next afternoon, Ayesha showed up at our front door, smiling. She looked the same as ever, her black hair in a high ponytail, five or six gold studs running up the edge of each ear like a constellation I couldn't identify. But it was weird how she was holding a small rhombus-shaped banana bread she said she'd baked herself—as if this were a social visit, which it wasn't.

"I can't promise you guys it's edible," she admitted, laughing. Mom brought the banana bread into the living room on a fancy plate. When she cut slices, we could see how the middle of the loaf looked gummy. So we ate the end pieces with our tea and traded hospital gossip—mostly about how one of the receptionists had married a nurse we all thought was cute. Then Ayesha told us she was moving in with her girlfriend; they were in love, she said, and very happy.

Mom and I made a fuss about how glad we were, then Mom announced that she had to go make a phone call, but I could tell she really just wanted to give us privacy. And I could tell Ayesha got it too, because as soon as Mom was out of the room, she sat all the way forward, her elbows on her thighs, her chin resting on her fists.

"Norah, you look incredible," she said. "You've gained weight, your hair is growing in, and I'm loving the earrings."

"Thanks. They're new, so I have to keep them in."

She nodded quickly, as if she was in a hurry to push the conversation forward. "So what's going on? I heard from your dad that you want to homeschool?"

"Yes," I said eagerly. "Exactly."

"Okay, but why? You told me school was going great."

"Yeah, basically. It's not about the work."

"So what's it about, then?"

"The people."

She smiled. "People are people. They're all over the place, you know? You can't escape them."

"Yeah, I know. But the problem is, no one at school understands me."

"*Literally* no one?"

"Well, okay, not literally. I mean, a few people do. Ish." I picked at the crust of my banana bread. "I have this guidance counselor who wants me to talk about 'overcoming challenges,' like I once had this problem, and yay for me, everybody, look how well I solved it. I'd *never* talk that way about being sick."

"Yeah, I can see that. What about the other kids?"

"All the seventh graders think I'm going to die any minute. Or they think I'm faking, or just asking for special attention, which is crazy. And the eighth graders—I tried to act normal with them, but I screwed up. Really badly. Actually, I screwed up in front of the whole school. So now *everyone* thinks I'm weird."

"Well, but you're in middle school. It's *about* feeling weird."

"But it's weirder for *me*."

"*Everyone* thinks it's weirder for them."

I groaned. "Come on, Ayesha. When you went back to school after cancer, it was really hard for you, right?"

"Are you kidding? Of course it was. Especially the first year. But I told myself: *Look, you beat cancer, you can deal with high school.* And I did."

"But what if I'd rather just homeschool with you? Couldn't we go back to that? Remember all the math we did? And the science experiments? And the Greek myths?"

"Of course I remember, Norah." She reached across to hold my hands. "But no. I'm very sorry."

I couldn't believe what she was saying. Maybe I was hearing it wrong. "We can't? Why not?"

"Because . . . well, the truth is, I'm not teaching anymore."

"You're not?" I pulled my hands away.

"I've switched careers," Ayesha said quietly. "I'm going to

nursing school now. To be a pediatric oncology nurse, maybe get a job at Phipps one day."

"Oh." It felt as if I'd just been snatched by Hades and dumped into the underworld.

Ayesha pouted, teasing me for my expression. "Aww, don't look so sad, Norah. Come on, aren't you happy for me?"

"Yeah. If that's what you want to do. But I thought—I mean, didn't you like teaching sick kids?"

She got up from her chair to hug me. "Norah, listen to me: I loved working with you. You were my best student—my favorite. But that was when you were sick. We can't go back to that; we can't go back to *anything*. All we can do is move forward, you know?"

"Ayesha, I *tried* to move forward," I wailed. "But I couldn't!"

"Then you need to try harder, okay? And you need to give other people a chance."

"To do what? *Understand?*" I said the word like it burned my mouth.

Ayesha went silent. Then she said, "Let me ask you something: Do you *want* people to understand?"

"Of course! Why wouldn't I?"

"Because maybe you like that a little bit, feeling that nobody gets what you've been through. I know that's how *I* felt for a very long time. I think I was angry with the universe for making me sick, and maybe also at other kids for *not* being sick. And then, one day, I guess I just got tired of being angry."

Now tears were streaming down my face. Snot, too, which I wiped with my hand.

Is Ayesha right—do I LIKE thinking no one understands?

Am I angry?

All right, maybe I am.

And why shouldn't I be? At everyone! My friends, my parents, my teachers. Even people at the hospital, including Ayesha, who was supposed to save me, not desert me!

Although it was funny how as soon as I had this thought, it popped like a big wet soap bubble. I wasn't being fair—Ayesha wasn't deserting me. She was just moving forward.

And she was right: I needed to move forward too.

At least *try to* move forward.

Try *harder*.

She pulled out a tissue from her purse. "Wipe," she said. "Blow."

I did.

Ayesha poked my elbow. "Hey, didn't you like my technique just then? Don't you think I'll make a rock-star nurse?"

I nodded. "You're a rock star at everything, Ayesha."

"Aww, what a sweet thing to say, Norah! Thank you!"

"Except baking," I added, sticking out my tongue.

WHOOSH

Nobody made me go to school on Wednesday. Ms. Castro called to see if there was anything she could do, but I told her there wasn't.

Then she said, "Well, Norah, I hope you'll return very soon. You've already triumphed over so much, so if you put your mind to it, I *know* you can succeed at Burr!"

I groaned inside my head. Ms. Castro was congratulating me again, acting like my leukemia (which she still wouldn't name!) was something I'd "triumphed over," a "challenge" I'd "overcome," like hiking up a vacation mountain. Why was I being so difficult when I had a problem I'd already solved?

It's all behind you now!

Woohoo!

After I finally got off the phone, I thought: *Okay, so maybe if Ayesha can't be my teacher, I'll just stay home and teach myself.*

You can learn anything online, right? And this way I'll never have to see Griffin again.

Because more and more, as the bake-sale incident replayed itself in my mind like a never-ending GIF, I realized that Griffin's face—his expression—was the most upsetting thing about it. If he hadn't "heard" about my secret before, he definitely heard about it right then. And in the worst possible way.

So there was nothing else to think except that I'd blown it with the first boy I'd ever crushed on. I'd never even shown him my kraken sketches, or told him what I'd decided about the norah: that her tentacles could transform into wings.

And now, of course, it was too late.

I was on the sofa, half napping, half reading one of my favorite stories—the one about Orpheus, the musician who followed his wife, Eurydice, into the underworld. Hades said Orpheus could rescue Eurydice—but only if, as he was leading her out of the underworld, he didn't look back. And guess what happened? Yep.

"Norah? Friend here to see you," Dad called from the foyer. I looked up, expecting Harper.

And I can't explain this, but right before the "friend" walked into the living room, something changed. It was feeling like *whoosh*—a sense that all the air molecules had shifted in a weird direction. So when I looked up and saw it was Griffin, my heart was already zooming.

"Hey," he said. His spiky hair looked messier than usual.

Probably from the wind, I thought, wondering if he'd walked all this way from school.

"Hi, Griffin," I said in a squeaky voice I didn't recognize. "Why are you here?"

He perched awkwardly on the edge of Dad's favorite chair. "Just to see what's going on. Are you okay?"

I swallowed. "Yeah. I *was* sick, but I'm better now."

"Good. So when are you coming back to school?"

I shrugged. "It's sort of complicated."

"No, it's not."

"What?" I stared at him.

"If you're all better, you should just come back," he said quietly. "Look, Norah, I know you were sick before. Before this year, I mean."

It felt like the floor was cracking underneath me. "You did? How did you—"

"Ezra said something once, but I didn't get it. And Astrid made some comment, but I never trust her. So I figured if it was true, you'd just tell me yourself. But after that bake-sale thing, I talked to Harper."

"Harper?"

"Astrid said you two were friends in Art Club. So that's why I gave Harper that note to give you."

Right, the note mummy.

And now my brain was whirling. Because I'd specifically told Harper I didn't want Griffin to know about my cancer!

So how could she talk about it behind my back?

Griffin rubbed his hair, messing it up even worse. "I didn't know you and Harper were both in the same grade. In *seventh* grade, I mean."

"Sorry. I was going to mention it, but—"

"Yeah, I was surprised, because you're so ahead of me in math. Anyway, Harper said you had leukemia. For two years."

"Yeah. I did."

"And?"

"And what?" There were glass shards in my throat. "What do you want me to say about it?"

"I don't know. How come you never mentioned it?"

"Griffin, I never lied to you or anyone else. I just . . . didn't talk about it."

"Why not?"

"Because I didn't want you to treat me like Cancer Girl! That's how everyone in the seventh grade acts toward me, and I *hate* it. So I thought if I didn't mention it—"

"It would just go away?"

"No. I mean, it can't. It never will. Even *if* I'm all better."

He didn't say anything. Then he asked: "So what *did* you think, then?"

"Just that *other* things about me were true. Like . . . the fact I read books. And draw creatures."

"Okay," Griffin said. He took a slow breath. "I get that, Norah. I do. But if I told you something important about myself, something personal, would you think, *Okay, that's ALL he's about, and nothing else*?"

"Of course not," I admitted.

"Well, that's kind of how you treated me."

My throat ached. I knew he was right; I was unfair to everybody.

But I couldn't talk, because if I did, the glass shards would just keep breaking.

Finally, though, I had to ask. "So what is it you'd tell me? I mean, if you were telling me something personal."

He scratched his nose. "Like, okay: Did you ever wonder why I just suddenly showed up here, in the eighth grade?"

"Yeah, actually."

"It's because my dad lost his job. And that meant we lost our house and had to move in with my grandmother."

"Oh. That's terrible," I said, thinking how it explained some stuff: the beat-up bass. Why he never had pens. Why he didn't still have a sign that said GRIFFIN DOOR.

"It's not great. I mean, it's not *cancer*, but . . ." He shrugged, smiling a little. "I miss my old friends, though."

"You can still keep in touch with them, right?"

"Yeah, but it's not the same. They have new stuff going on. But so do I, I guess. Anyhow." He got up. "I have to go now."

"Why?" I blurted. "I mean, you don't have to."

"No, I do. We're having band rehearsal at Rowan's house. But I ducked out. I told them I forgot my phone, so."

"Well, thanks for coming here."

"I'd rather see you at school, Norah." He peeked at me through his eyelashes. "Also Afterschool."

Without saying good-bye, he turned and left.

Again I had the feeling of *whoosh*.

PERSEPHONE

The minute Griffin left, my brain leapt from *No way I'm ever going back*

  to: *Okay, so what if I DID go back?*

to: *How can I POSSIBLY go back, after missing so much time?*

to: *Hey, Norah, you already missed two whole years, what's the big deal about another few days?*

I called Harper that night. Already I'd forgotten my first instinct—to yell at her for telling Griffin about my cancer. Now I was glad he knew. No, not glad—relieved.

"Have you started the Greek myth speeches in English?" I asked her.

"No," she said. I could tell she was grinning. "Ms. Farrell is meeting with us one-on-one to hear what we're planning. Some people have started writing, but not me."

"Okay, good."

"So . . . does that mean you're coming back to school?"

"Yeah, actually. I'll see you tomorrow."

"Yay!" She was jumping; I could tell.

"Harper?"

"Yes?"

"Thanks for hanging with me in that stinky bathroom. Aria, too."

"Anytime." She laughed. "But don't make us do it again, okay?"

The next morning, Mom and Dad both came to drop me off at school, and to have another meeting with Ms. Castro about my "adjustment issues," or something. I didn't ask, because I knew I'd be hearing about it later from my parents. Possibly even from Ms. Castro. And if she summoned me to her office, there was no way to avoid going.

I went to homeroom. Right away Cait and Aria came running over, as if they hadn't seen me in forever.

"We thought you weren't coming back," Cait said.

"So did I," I admitted. "But I couldn't stay away from *that*." I pointed to Malik and Harrison, who were giving each other noogies. "So what's been happening?"

Aria and Cait exchanged glances.

"What?" I asked.

"Well," Aria said, "the big news is that Kylie and Silas got suspended."

"Omigod, really? What for?"

"Remember when they left the building to get pizza?"

You mean when Kylie left the building and Silas followed her, the idiot. "Yeah."

"They did it again," Cait said, her eyes bulging. "Only this time, they left for the whole rest of the day. So now they're both in major trouble."

I shook my head. Kylie was Kylie, but Silas was still Silas. Something had happened to make him follow her like a stupid puppy, but maybe it was possible to remind him about the kid he used to be. Even if we weren't friends anymore, I knew I should try. Besides, hadn't Harper said he'd wanted to talk to me? In the blur of the last few weeks, I'd lost track of people.

Not Griffin, though. As soon as I saw him in first period math, I had a feeling like: *Okay. This friendship—or relationship, whatever I'm supposed to call it—is important to me, and I do NOT want to mess it up.*

So the first thing I said to him was: "Griffin, you're right: I should have told you things. I'm very sorry."

"Nothing to apologize for," he replied. Then he grinned. "Except not showing me those sketches like you promised."

I reached into my backpack and took out a folder that had my three best kraken sketches. "Voila," I said, putting them on his desk. "My favorite is the one with the spikes, but it's your logo, so you decide."

"Whoa!" he cried. "Norah, they're all amazing! *You're* amazing."

Then we both got too embarrassed to keep talking.

* * *

"Norah, good to see you!" Ms. Farrell greeted me. "We need to talk about your speech. Give me three minutes, and then you and I can chat."

She scurried off to talk to Addison and Malik, leaving the fancy-soap smell behind her.

"Do you know which character you're doing?" Harper asked. She was so happy I was back that she couldn't stop smiling.

I didn't even have to think. "Yep. Persephone."

"The one who got kidnapped by Hades?"

"Yeah. And rescued by her mom. But then she had to go back to the underworld half of the year because she ate the pomegranate."

Harper nodded thoughtfully. "You know, I never understood that part."

"You mean why she ate it, if it was the food of the dead?"

"Yeah," Harper said. "Was she just stress eating, maybe?"

"Maybe." The truth was, I hadn't thought very hard about that detail either. It was definitely strange: If Persephone hated being in the underworld so much, why would she eat a fruit that meant she could never leave?

"All right." Ms. Farrell had returned to my desk. "Norah, so that we don't disturb Harper, who needs to be finishing up her first draft"—she raised her eyebrows at Harper's nearly empty page—"why don't you and I relocate?"

I followed Ms. Farrell to the back wall, where there were two chairs set up for "conferencing."

"So," she said. "First of all, Norah: I'd just like to say I'm delighted to see you back at school. Anything you ever need, any time you'd like to chat about *anything*—"

"Thank you," I said. It was the first time I'd said those words without trying to end the conversation. Ms. Farrell was a great teacher, I thought, so smart about things, and not fake-understanding. And I loved the fact that today she was wearing a Beowulf tee.

She smiled. "So you've chosen your character, I hope?"

When I told her yes, I'd chosen Persephone, she asked why.

"I just really like that myth," I said, shrugging. "It's always been my favorite."

"Okay, but the project is not about *liking* a myth, or a particular character. It's about empathy, remember? You need to do it first person, feeling Persephone's emotions, thinking her thoughts. Do you think you can relate to her that way?"

I was prepared for this. "Oh, definitely! Because of the way Hades and Demeter fight over her. It's like how my mom and dad compete over me."

But as soon as I said this answer, I thought: *Except not anymore. Not really.* The truth was, ever since that time Mom stuck up for Nicole, everyone had been getting along okay. Nicole wasn't avoiding our house all the time. Mom and Dad had stopped trying to make me choose sides. They'd even stopped competing about who was a better nurse.

So why *did* I like this myth so much, anyway? Why did I feel this strong connection to Persephone?

Ms. Farrell tucked some loose wisps of hair behind her ear. "Okay, Norah," she said. "I know you'll do a great speech. But I hope you'll keep thinking about that story."

"What do you mean?" I felt almost scared, as if my teacher had just read my mind.

"I just mean dig deeper. Don't go with the obvious. Ask yourself if there's more there for you to say. More to connect with."

"Like what?"

"Just keep thinking." She smiled, pressed her hand on my shoulder, and walked off to talk to Cait.

THE DOG

The rest of the day, I tried not to think about what Ms. Farrell meant. But I couldn't shake the suspicion that once again, she was asking me to be Cancer Girl, turning the whole Persephone myth into a story about My Leukemia.

And here was the funny thing: I wasn't even mad this time. A few things had happened—the bake sale disaster, seeing Ayesha again, that conversation with Griffin at my house—to make something shift inside of me, somehow. Now I didn't think, *How dare Ms. Farrell force me to give a speech about something private! Something nobody in the class can understand!* I thought: *What did she mean about digging deeper? Is there something about the myth—which I've read more than a zillion times—that I'm not getting?* It seemed impossible.

And yet:

Persephone had been playing in the meadow, innocently gathering flowers, when out of the blue the earth cracked beneath her, and she got sucked down to the underworld. Which, the more I thought about it, was a bit like getting cancer. Because two years ago, there I was, minding my own business, going to school, hanging out with Harper and Silas, when BOOM. The earth cracked open, and down I fell.

And Phipps was sort of like the underworld, in a way. I mean, all the people there were extremely nice, especially Dr. Glickstein, Raina, and Ayesha. But being there still felt like being Nowhere, especially in the middle of the night. And the chemo drugs were awful, even if they saved my life.

And now here I was, rescued, back on earth with Demeter. (And Dad, who I guessed was Zeus? Although he only had one girlfriend.) All of that made sense to me. But if there was more to say about that myth, more to connect with, more that had to do *with me*, I didn't see it. So I couldn't imagine what Ms. Farrell wanted, why she wasn't satisfied.

At dismissal, Dad was waiting for me in his car.

"Where's Mom?" I asked as I slid into the passenger seat. I knew she'd changed her plan to go back to California right away, but other details were still fuzzy.

"Actually, she's interviewing," Dad said. "At Columbia University."

I screamed. "You mean *for a job*? Back here, in the city?"

"Yep. The bicoastal family thing has been very hard on her. She wants to live closer to her beloved offspring."

My mouth dropped open. "Omigod, that's incredible! I'm so happy! Why didn't she tell me?"

"Because she's convinced she won't get hired. But your mom is a brilliant teacher, and *I'm* convinced she will. Nicole's even making a celebratory dinner tonight."

"She is? For Mom?"

"Yep." He reached over to pat my knee. "Also for you."

"Me? What did I do?"

"You went back to school today, didn't you? We know it hasn't been easy, and we're all so proud of our tough girl. How did it go?"

I told him about the speech project, how Ms. Farrell wanted me to "dig deeper" into the Persephone myth, but I felt like I'd already struck the bottom.

"Maybe pick a different myth?" Dad suggested.

I was horrified. "No, Dad! I absolutely *have* to do Persephone! It's *my myth*!"

"Hmm. Well, if it's your myth, don't give up on it, then."

We turned the corner onto Maple Avenue. And maybe if Mom had been in the car to enforce the No-After-School-Socializing rule, I wouldn't have said anything. But it was just Dad and me—and I'd always had the feeling he was a little calmer about the Parent Rules. So I asked if we could stop at Silas's house, which was the next block over.

"Silas?" Dad repeated. "I thought you two weren't such good friends lately."

"We're not. I just need to yell at him about something."

"I don't know, Norah. You heard what Dr. Choi said about needing your rest—"

"Five minutes! Please, Dad? I'll talk to Silas really fast!"

He grunted. "Five minutes. And if you're not out in five, I'm honking my horn."

I got out of the car and ran up the driveway to Silas's house, a place I'd been a million times, although never in the last two years. Nothing about it seemed different, although when I rang the doorbell, a dog started barking inside. Silas had a dog now? This was new.

The door opened. Silas was holding a squirming shaggy gray dog by the collar.

"Oh," he said, startled to see me. "Hi."

I didn't bother smiling. "Can I come in for a sec? My dad's waiting."

"Sure." Wrestling with the dog to keep it from jumping on me, he led me into his kitchen, where the TV was blaring.

"You got a new dog," I said brilliantly.

"Actually, Jasper belongs to my grandparents, and he pees all over the place. What's up?"

"Not much. I heard you got suspended."

"Yeah. I can't go back to school until next Monday."

"Silas, what's going on with you? You keep letting Kylie get you into trouble."

He released Jasper, who ran over to sniff my jeans. "I don't care," he said. "It's worth it."

"How can that *possibly* be true?"

"I just really like her." He was blushing so hard I had to look away. "Like you like that new kid, Griffin."

My stomach dropped. "What? Silas, where did you—how do you even know about that?"

He shrugged. "Everyone knows. It's not a secret. So anyway, you should understand."

"Actually, I don't! Because the situations are completely different! Griffin is a really sweet person. But Kylie doesn't care *one bit* about you—"

"That's your opinion. In *my* opinion, she's beautiful."

"Silas, I never said she was *ugly*!"

"I even wrote a song for her. You want to hear it?"

"NO THANKS."

"Well, you'll hear it in school. I'm doing it for my speech."

I felt like bopping him. But what good would it do? Silas was hopelessly in love. And I'd read enough Greek myths to know that love could make you stupid.

I petted Jasper's shaggy head. "Anyway, Harper said you wanted to talk to me?"

"Yeah. You want a glass of water? Or some soda?" He opened his refrigerator door and stared inside, as if he was searching for something. But then he closed the door empty-handed.

I could tell he was stalling for some reason, and that made me nervous. "So what did you want to talk *about*?"

"Um. Well, all right." He hugged his arms like he was shielding his body from attack. "It's about why I never visited you in the hospital."

"You already told me that, didn't you? You said you wanted to, but you couldn't. Whatever *that's* supposed to mean."

"Yeah. I know how it sounds." He didn't say anything for a few seconds. I could hear Jasper chewing something in the living room, and also the humming of the refrigerator. And just when I thought these noises would be the end of the conversation, he said:

"Hey, Norah. Remember that dumb game we used to play? On our bikes?"

I shrugged. "You mean the one with the evil elves? And how we'd have to ride around finding magic crap to break their spells?"

"Yeah. I was thinking about it the other day when I was putting out the garbage. It was so dumb."

"I know."

"But also really fun."

"Okay."

"And I was thinking how nice it was, just riding around the neighborhood. We did that every afternoon, didn't we?"

"Uh-huh." *What does this have to do with anything?*

"And I guess that's how I still think of you, on your bike. I know it's stupid of me, okay? But when you got sick, and I knew you didn't look like that anymore, and maybe you wouldn't be okay, or just not, you know, *riding your bike*, I couldn't . . ." He shook his head helplessly. "It just felt like you were done with the game, but I wasn't."

A loud honking sound, which I knew was Dad.

Was this it? Was Silas finished with his big explanation? He hadn't told me anything I didn't know.

But he was right about one thing: I *was* done with our game. And maybe that wasn't only because I'd gotten sick.

"Have to go," I said.

Silas's head drooped. Then his shoulders started shaking, and I could tell he was crying. I didn't know what else to do, so I gave him a piece of paper towel. To hand it to him I had to get up close—close enough to get a whiff of his laundry detergent. I'd always liked the scent of his clothes—just chemicals, I knew, but now a smell memory of the little kid I used to hang out with.

Poor Silas, I thought. *This was so hard for him.*

Not as hard as for ME. But still.

He's really such a baby.

He dried his eyes. "Ugh. Don't tell anyone."

"Don't worry, I'm the World Not-Talking Champion."

That was when Jasper peed on my sneaker.

"Jasper! Bad!" Silas shouted. "Sorry, Norah. He's mad that my grandparents are on vacation."

I shook my foot. "Maybe he needs to go out."

Silas groaned. "He *always* needs to go out."

"Do you walk him?"

"I guess. Some."

"Let's go walk him together."

"Now?"

"Yeah," I said.

Silas and Jasper followed me out of the house. We went over to Dad, who rolled down his window.

"Hey there, Silas," he said. "Long time, no see."

"Dad," I said, meeting his eyes. "Silas and I are going to take his grandparents' dog for a walk. I know you want me to go home and rest, but this is *very, very important.* I could have just snuck out the back door, but I promised not to freak you out again by disappearing, so I'm telling you *exactly* where I'm going. I'll be home in an hour. Okay?"

I held my breath, ready for an argument. But I think Dad saw something in our faces, or heard something in my voice.

Also, at that moment, Jasper put his front paws on Dad's window, and drooled.

"Okay," Dad said, waved at us, and backed out of the driveway.

POMEGRANATE

When I got home exactly one hour later, the house smelled like hot fruit. Maybe Nicole was baking a pie, I thought, my mouth watering as I entered the kitchen.

"Hey, girl." Nicole barely looked up at me as she whisked something in a small saucepan.

"Hi," I said, poking my nose into a saucepan, where red juice was bubbling. "What are you making?"

"Pomegranate Chicken. An ancient Persian dish, extremely yummy."

I stared at her. *"Pomegranate?"*

"Uh-huh. Don't tell me you've never had pomegranate seeds." She held up a bowl of tiny red seeds, small glistening rubies that looked almost poisonous.

"No," I replied. Because I thought it was the food of the dead! Not an actual, literal *thing to eat*, just something in a myth, like ambrosia or manna. But with bad associations, especially for Persephone. "I think I once had a pomegranate-flavored lollipop or something. But I never ate the real fruit. How does it taste?"

"Delicious! But hands off those seeds; I need them for my recipe." Nicole seemed jumpy as she shooed me out of the kitchen. Was she nervous about cooking for Mom? Why would she be? She wasn't planning to poison her, was she?

Norah, this isn't a myth; stop it, I scolded myself. *Mom and Nicole are getting along just fine!*

Nicole poked my arm. "All right, I'm busy, so don't distract me now, please. Go wash up and set the table, okay?"

"Sure."

While I was upstairs in the bathroom, the doorbell rang. I could hear Mom's voice as she came in, and then a happy cheer from Dad, followed by a loud cheer from Nicole. All the cheering made it sound as if Mom got the job. I did a little dance with elbows.

But here's the strange part: Instead of going straight into the living room to give Mom a hug, I snuck into the kitchen. I absolutely *had* to taste those pomegranate seeds, even though Nicole needed them for her recipe.

Because the more I thought about the Persephone myth—and I'd thought about it the whole walk home from Silas's—the more I was convinced that the pomegranate was the key. *D'Aulaires'* said Persephone ate the pomegranate seeds while "lost in thought." Stress eating, Harper had called it.

But that didn't make any sense. Persephone wasn't a zombie—she'd know when she was eating something, especially after going so long without food. And if the fruit was so delicious, she'd taste it, right? Ayesha once told me about this other version, where Hades tricks Persephone into eating the pomegranate seeds, but that wasn't any more believable. I mean, if she was already eating *other* stuff, maybe he could sneak a few seeds into the recipe—but she wasn't eating *anything*, period. So how could she not realize she was eating the pomegranate?

While the red liquid simmered in the saucepan, the unused pomegranate seeds were still on the counter in a small bowl. I grabbed a handful of juicy seeds and stuffed them into my mouth, half expecting the kitchen floor to open, and me to get sucked into the crevice.

Nothing happened.

The seeds were delicious, tart, a little like raspberry—but more like the lollipop version of raspberry than the actual fruit. And there was another flavor, a deeper one, in the background. What was it? I couldn't figure it out, so I grabbed another handful.

"Norah?" Suddenly Nicole was behind me.

I spun around, flailing my arm, which crashed into the saucepan handle, sending the whole thing to the floor. *Splat.*

"Oh, no! Oh, Nicole, I'm so sorry!" Frantically, I grabbed

some paper towels and tried to sop up the red juice. "Maybe if we squeeze it out—"

Nicole crouched beside me with a sponge. "No. It's just gone. That's okay."

"But it's not! I feel terrible! You were making something special for us, for *Mom*, and you told me not to eat your pomegranate, so I had no business—"

Nicole put her hand on my arm and smiled, showing the gap between her front teeth. "You wanted a taste. It's not a crime; don't be so hard on yourself. It's just food, silly."

We had a great dinner anyway. Nicole used the few extra pomegranate seeds left in the bowl, combined them with apples, oranges, and lemons she found in the bin of our refrigerator, and invented a fruity sauce for the chicken. Even Mom had to admit it was delicious; she didn't snark once about Nicole being a "foodie."

The whole time, we talked about Mom's new job. It would start in the spring, she said, and it was "probationary," which meant that basically it was a tryout. ("But what job isn't?" she said, laughing.) For now, Mom needed to return to California, settle things in her lab, pack her apartment. When she said she'd be back here around Thanksgiving, Nicole shouted, "You'd better be! Because I'm cooking!"

"You'd *better* be cooking," Mom replied, and Dad laughed.

So did I. Our family was weird, pretty much the opposite

of a Greek myth. No poison fruit, no thunderbolts, no curses or spells. All the grown-ups were friends—Mom and Dad, Mom and Nicole. However it had happened (and it must have been sometime when I wasn't looking), I was really glad about how we were all getting along.

Also about Mom's new job, and the fact she'd be living close by. When Dad brought out a bottle of wine and the grown-ups clinked glasses, I clinked my water.

"Here's to only good things from now on," Dad said. "For all of us."

"Only good things," Mom agreed, glancing at me with wet eyes.

"Only good things," Nicole repeated, smiling at everyone.

But that's impossible, I thought. *You can't have only good things.*

And that was when I had my speech. It came to me at the dinner table fully written, like a gift from the gods.

OMIGODS: SPEECH DAY IN MS. FARRELL'S SECOND PERIOD ENGLISH CLASS

Cait (speaking while signing in American Sign Language): "Hello, my name is Echo. I'm using sign language because Hera took away my ability to speak my own thoughts. But I still have opinions, and there are a few things I need to say.

"First, to Hera: I'm sorry I distracted you when you came to the woods looking for Zeus. I now know he was having an affair with one of the nymphs, but I swear to you I didn't know it then. I didn't distract you on purpose, I just couldn't keep my mouth shut. Not being able to speak my own thoughts anymore is a terrible curse—and honestly, I don't deserve it. If you would let me speak my own words again, I'll praise you all day long, I'll tell you stories and jokes, I promise not to make bad puns or waste my breath on silly comments or gossip. Please, please lift your curse and let me speak like myself again. Repeating other people's words all day is driving me crazy. I bet it's driving everyone else crazy too.

"Second, Pan: I like you as a friend. But only as a friend. Please respect my feelings and BACK OFF.

"Third, Narcissus: You are the earth's most beautiful male creature, and I'm madly in love with you. Why won't you even look at me? I'm not ugly—ask Pan, who won't leave me alone. It's so unfair how you never notice me, even though I'm always right behind you. I know I may seem like a creepy stalker—but maybe if you'd stop looking at yourself for just one minute and notice *me*, I wouldn't need to follow you around, repeating your words. Anyway, if I don't get my own voice back, maybe we can sing love duets together. You have a nice voice—so that means I have a nice voice too."

Malik (carrying a beachball): "You know who I am? I'm Sisyphus, the guy rolling this rock uphill every day. Every night it rolls back down and then I have to start over, so you're probably wondering why I bother. Believe me, a lot of the time so do I. I'm told it's a punishment for my days as King of Corinth, when I was mighty and powerful and kept on tricking the gods. Whatever. I'm hoping that one day I'll be King of Corinth again, but until then, I try to stay positive. At least I have this busy-work to keep me in shape. Beats working out on a treadmill, right?"

Harper (covered in fake Halloween-decoration cobwebs): "My name is Arachne. I know the story you've heard about me: I'm this obnoxious mortal girl who went around bragging about being the best weaver on earth. But that's an exaggeration. I never said I was the best; I just really, really love to weave, and I'm incredibly good at it. There's nothing wrong with taking pride in your work, is there? But Athena is so bossy and stuck-up, and she always overreacts whenever she feels someone is challenging her powers, which I would never do. Because (hello!) she's a goddess—so when she challenged me to a weaving contest, I had no choice. (Yes, I know you probably heard that *I* challenged *Athena*, but why would I? I'm not an idiot.) Anyway, it was so unfair how she ripped up my tapestry just because she didn't like the scene I wove. Maybe she didn't like my choice of subject (and I admit depicting Zeus's twenty-one infidelities was a bit edgy on my part), but that didn't mean it was bad! And turning me into a spider? Total overreaction."

Silas (strumming a guitar):
"Eurydice, my beautiful wife
This is Orpheus singing
To guide you back to life.
Don't think about our wedding
When you got bitten by that snake
And had to go to the underworld
Instead of eating wedding cake.
You are my one true love,
My soul mate and my double—

I'll follow you even if

It gets me into trouble."

Aria (in camouflage vest and orange hunting cap, carrying bow and arrow): "Yo, Actaeon, I'm talking to you! This is Artemis! I don't know how you didn't get the message, but everyone else on earth knows that I'm not into boys. Or girls, for that matter! I'm totally focused on my career as goddess of the hunt, so get over your infatuation NOW. And stop staring at me, because it's really creepy! Oh, and another thing: If you ever spy on me again when I'm bathing in the woods, you're going to be frolicking with Thumper full-time, get it?"

Addison (wearing tiara): "I'm Hera, and I want a divorce."

Kylie (with smashed-up wings made out of pipe cleaners, and wet hair): "Hey, guys, it's Icarus, and yeah, I know I screwed up. My dad Daedalus (who I call Daddalus) made these really cool wings for me to escape our prison, and I guess I got a little carried away (literally, haha). Anyway, what happened was, I flew too close to the sun, my wings melted, and I drowned. But omigods—lesson learned. So don't be so hard on me, okay?"

Harrison (with toy stethoscope around his neck): "I am Asclepius, god of medicine. My father was Apollo, god of sun, light, music, poetry, the arts, archery, and healing. I specialize in one thing: medicine. That may sound boring, but Dad's life had way too much drama. If you ask me, medicine should be boring. Because when it's interesting, that means someone's sick."

Me: "My name is Persephone. About two years ago, I was snatched away from my happy life and taken to the underworld. I didn't ask for it, and I didn't do anything to deserve it. I don't know why Hades fell in love with me, but he did. The whole time he kept me a prisoner in the underworld, I was incredibly lonely and bored—so bored I thought I'd go crazy. Fortunately, the underworld has a big library, so at least I could catch up on my reading.

"But every day I was in the underworld, all I dreamed about was returning to earth. Sometimes in the middle of the night I'd wake up and start to freak out—because I couldn't remember where I was, or how I'd gotten there. And the only way I could get through the night was by thinking about my room back home, and about my parents, Demeter and Zeus. They're not together anymore, but I knew they both still loved me.

"My mom, Demeter, goddess of the hearth and the harvest, had to give up her work to search for me, but she didn't care. She refused to give up—and when she told my dad, Zeus, what had happened to me, he got just as upset, and was just as determined to get me back. So he sent Hermes to fetch me from the underworld. Hades was an evil, powerful god, but even he had to listen when Zeus said I should be released.

"But when Hermes arrived in the underworld, this gardener told him that I'd eaten the food of the dead—so I was 'of the underworld' and couldn't return to earth.

"Okay. Now my story gets a little complicated. In one version, the gardener said that he found six pomegranate seeds missing, and that I ate them because I was 'lost in thought.'

"In another version, Hades tricked me into eating the pomegranate seeds.

"Either way, I messed up, right? I ate the pomegranate without meaning to, without realizing I was doing it, but that's no excuse. I still ate the food of the dead. And that meant I had to spend half of my life back in the underworld.

"Well, what I need to tell you is that both of those versions are wrong. When I ate those pomegranate seeds, it wasn't a mistake or an accident; I did it on purpose. Just as Hermes came to get me, to bring me back home to earth, I stuffed six seeds into my mouth. I knew what I was doing.

"I know what you're thinking: *But* why? *Why would you do that, Persephone? You hated* every single second *you were in the underworld. All you ever dreamed about was returning to earth, having a normal life again. So why would you eat* the one food *that would mean things would* never *be completely normal for you, that you'd have to return to the underworld for six whole months of every year, forever?*

"This is why: When Hermes came to get me, he said Zeus and Demeter were planning to erase all my memories of the underworld. The underworld was all behind me now, Hermes said. 'Only good things from now on.'

"Well, I refused to accept that. Because after living in the underworld all that time, it became part of me, part of who I am. I could finally go back to the earth, I *wanted* to go back to the earth, I wanted to hug Demeter and pick flowers, and do all the normal, regular girl stuff, just like I had before the dark day Hades kidnapped me. But to erase all my memories of the underworld, and pretend that everything was the same as it used to be, would be a lie. I mean, I couldn't pretend I didn't know what the underworld is like. I couldn't tell myself that only good things will be in my future, because how could you be sure of that, anyhow? And having been in the underworld—surviving all that time—made me tough. Made me realize I could survive anything in existence, including evil gods and monsters. So I never *wanted* to forget that.

"The underworld is real. It's not like it goes away just because you're back on earth. It's always there, part of the whole big universe. And now I knew that.

"The other thing was, I was scared. I know that probably sounds crazy, but it's the truth: I was scared to go back to the beautiful earth. Because I couldn't stop worrying: What if no one understood what had happened to me? What if, the whole time I was away, everything had changed? Or what if the earth hadn't changed at all, but I had? Maybe I'd moved forward, and couldn't go back.

"The underworld was horrible. But if you live anywhere for a long time, it feels like home, I guess. So I think I was scared to give it up, or maybe just not ready.

"Anyway, for all of those reasons, I ate the pomegranate.

BARBARA DEE

"Don't ask me what it tasted like. I can't explain. If you haven't tasted something, you can't really ask someone else to describe the flavor. You have to taste it yourself, but truthfully, I hope you never do.

"Just know that I ate it on purpose. I wasn't only a sort of victim, getting kidnapped and rescued. I wasn't sleepwalking and I wasn't tricked. I made a decision; I acted. And here I am."

LOCH NESS MONSTER

After I finished, the room went quiet. So I thought I'd blown it.

But when I sat down, Harper gave me a hug, and Aria poked me. "Norah, you crushed that thing like a grape," she whispered. "Like a *grape*."

We voted on the three best. At the end of class, Ms. Farrell announced the winners: Aria, Cait, and me. I was the only unanimous vote getter—which meant that everyone in the class had voted for me. Even Addison, weirdly enough.

Ms. Farrell said that we'd be presenting the speeches in a school assembly next week, and Aria, Cait, and I could invite any-one we wanted, not just parents. I knew exactly who I wanted to invite, but before I did, I had to ask Ms. Farrell a question.

So when class was over, I went up to her desk. "This isn't

part of that Overcoming Challenges thing, right?"

Ms. Farrell looked surprised. "Why? Would it be a problem if it was?"

I wasn't sure. A few weeks ago I'd have said yes without even thinking. Now I just shrugged.

All of a sudden, Addison was squeezing me in a hug. "Norah, that was so, so good!"

"Thanks," I said. I couldn't tell if she meant it—if she'd changed her mind about being jealous, or whatever she was. But as I watched her walk away, I realized I didn't care.

"Ms. Farrell?" Now Aria was in front of me, bouncing. "When I do Artemis onstage, is it okay if I shoot my arrow?"

"Absolutely not!" Ms. Farrell said. She looked horrified.

"But how come? I promise not to aim it at anyone!"

"Aria, it's a weapon! We're not taking the chance that your hand slips."

"I can still bring it with me onstage, right? If I don't shoot it?"

"I'll discuss it with the principal."

"Aww," Aria said, pouting. But Ms. Farrell wasn't Mrs. Maldonado, and this time I doubted she'd get her way.

Then Harper and Cait joined us.

"You both did great," I told them truthfully.

"Thanks," Harper replied as we hugged, "but I'm glad I didn't win, because I'd be too nervous to do it onstage. Although I'm kind of sorry Astrid won't hear it!"

I laughed. "Just say it in Art Club. We'll pretend you're rehearsing!"

"Yeah, Norah, let's totally do that!" Harper was laughing too, so I couldn't tell if she was serious. But I was.

Then Cait, who wasn't laughing, said, "Um, Ms. Farrell? I'm not sure about the assembly."

"What aren't you sure about?" Ms. Farrell asked patiently.

"The whole thing. If I can do it."

"Well, your classmates think you can," Ms. Farrell said. "No one's forcing you, Cait, but they did choose you to represent the class."

Aria put her arm around Cait's shoulders. "Come on, Caitie, you'll do amazing! Your speech rocked! How do you know sign language?"

"My little brother is deaf," Cait said. "That's how we talk at home."

"Omigosh, that's so cool! I wish *I* knew sign language!"

"Me too," Harper said.

"Me three," I said.

"I could teach you guys some words," Cait offered shyly. "Maybe next weekend, at my house?"

"Yes! And we'll sleep over," Aria declared.

"Aria, don't just invite yourself like that," Harper scolded, smacking her arm.

"No, no, that sounds fun," Cait protested happily. She turned to me. "Norah, you'll sleep over too?"

I grinned. "Yes. Definitely. That'll be awesome."

I knew it meant declaring war on the Weekend Rule—but I was ready for that fight.

I didn't have to wait long.

The next day, Saturday, I was reading on the sofa when the doorbell rang. Dad answered, and a couple of seconds later, *whoosh*. The air molecules shifted.

"Hey, Norah," Griffin said. He was smiling shyly, his hair sticking up at a weird angle, a small red zit on his chin. But I still thought he was the cutest boy I'd ever seen, and seeing him in my living room again just made my heart explode.

"Hi," I said in a chirpy voice. "What's up?"

"I have a present for you." He handed me a black tee. With my logo printed on it, and the word KRAKEN in slimy-looking letters. "We had these printed and they just arrived, so I thought you should have one."

I screamed.

Dad came running into the living room with a pale, freaked-out look on his face. "Norah, you okay?"

"LOOK," I said, holding up the tee. "MY LOGO."

"That's why you screamed?"

"YES. THAT'S WHY I SCREAMED."

Griffin was laughing behind his hand.

Dad stared at me. Then he stared at Griffin. "Oh," he said, the color returning to his face. "You shouldn't scare me like that, Norah."

"Sorry, I didn't mean to. Dad?"

"Yes?"

I peeked at Griffin. For the last couple of days, we'd been talking about a movie that had just come out, *Return to Loch Ness*. It was the sort of movie that was either extremely cool or so bad it was hilarious, but we couldn't tell from the online trailer. And when I'd mentioned to Griffin that I wanted to see it, he'd replied, "Yeah, we definitely should."

We. Which had to mean something, right?

"Griffin and I were wondering if you'd drive us to a movie," I said very fast.

Griffin coughed, or possibly choked. I couldn't tell which.

"Today?" Dad asked. "Now?" *In violation of the Resting-on-Weekends rule?* his eyes asked me.

Not in violation, my eyes answered. *Because I'm communicating with you! And it's time we got rid of that stupid thing, okay?*

Yeah, Dad agreed. *Okay.*

I looked at Griffin. "Unless you have something else to do right now?"

"Nah," he said, sticking his hands in his pockets. "Now is fine."

So I put on the kraken tee, Dad drove us to the mall, and we saw the movie. Not as a date, specifically—although not as a nondate, either. Just a griffin and a norah watching a screen together, sharing a tub of popcorn.

Oh, and by the way, the movie was hilarious.

UNDERWORLD

ive days later, I gave my Persephone speech for the
whole school. Dad and Nicole sat in the front row, Face-
Timing it with Mom so she could watch from California.
Raina and Ayesha sat right behind them, and when I finished,
the four of them gave me a loud, whooping standing ovation.
It was a bit embarrassing, like they were all wearing tees that
said NORAH'S TEAM—but a bunch of kids in the audience
stood, too: Harper and Silas, Malik, Griffin (of course), even
Kylie and Addison.

When it was over, Ms. Castro smothered me in a hug.
"Norah, I can't even tell you," she said. "I'm just speechless."

"Didn't she do a great job?" Ms. Farrell demanded. "Could
she have expressed it any better?"

"Absolutely not," Ms. Castro said. "Norah, the way you used
that story to capture your experience—"

"You mean *my cancer*?" I interrupted.

Ms. Castro looked like I'd peed on her shoe. "Yes, of course. Your cancer. Exactly."

And I thought: *Woohoo, she said the word. Victory at last!*

A couple of weeks later, it was time for my checkup at Phipps. By then Mom was back in New York, still staying with her friend Lisa but apartment-hunting for a place near Columbia University. Dad was out in Cleveland, interviewing some basketball player, so Mom took me to the hospital herself. On the train, which I hadn't been on in over two years. I couldn't stop smiling as I looked out the windows.

"When we're done at Phipps, I'm taking you earring shopping," Mom announced. "Do you have something specific in mind?"

I almost told her big fat dangly ones. But by then my hair was almost normal, so I didn't need the earrings to distract people. "I'm not sure," I admitted.

She grinned. "Ooh, good. That's always the most fun kind of shopping."

My checkup zoomed. All my tests were great. I'd gained six pounds. Raina couldn't stop gushing about my Persephone speech—she'd videoed it too, and shown it to all the doctors.

The only bad part was when we were in the waiting room, before we saw Dr. Glickstein. Mom went off to get her coffee, and while I sat there on the sofa, watching the sickest kids waiting for their tests, I saw the girl with the bandana and the BAD HAIR DAY tee. It took everything for me not to jump up from the sofa to tell her: *A few months ago I was as sick as you. And now I gave a speech in front of the entire school, I have a sort-of boyfriend, my hair is growing in, and I'm learning sign language with my friends! If I can do all that, so can you!*

But if I said these words, would they sound like Martian?

Probably yes. Maybe there were better words, a language we could both speak, but I didn't know what that would be.

When I got home that evening, I put on the new earrings in front of my mirror: pretty silver starfish that gleamed when I turned my head.

I was so lucky, I told myself. Lucky me.

Still, I couldn't stop thinking about the kids in the waiting room, who probably felt like the unluckiest kids on earth. Or rather, in the underworld, waiting for their rescue.

I couldn't rescue them, of course.

I couldn't do anything.

I couldn't even tell them about how *I'd* gotten rescued, because what difference would it make to *them*?

Except I did have one idea. One tiny little seed of an idea.

"Mom?" I said. She was in the kitchen, starting supper, a yummy-looking cheese omelet. "Could we possibly go back to Phipps?"

Her face paled. "Are you okay?"

Gah. I had to remember to stop freaking out my parents. But also, my parents needed to stop freaking out.

"I'm *completely fine*," I said. "I was just thinking there was something I wanted to do."

"At the hospital? Oh, you mean like a support group? Raina had mentioned one—"

"Not that."

I told her my idea, and she hugged me. "Let me make a few calls," she said.

Two days later, when Dad was back from his trip, they both took me to the hospital. They left me in the waiting room and said they'd be back in an hour.

I sat at a table with my book and my notebook. I opened my notebook, took out my purple gel pen, and drew a griffin. Then a norah. A kraken. A Hydra. A mini Charybdis. Then a squiggly monster who didn't have a name.

"What are you doing?" A small boy was standing next to me, watching. He was bald and very thin. He pointed to my norah. "What's that?"

"Me," I said. "Want me to draw you?"

He shrugged.

I drew a smiling shaggy monster with googly eyes. The boy grinned.

"Do you like cool stories?" I asked.

"Yeah," he said.

"About monsters and superheroes?"

He nodded.

"Want to hear one?"

He nodded even bigger.

I pulled out a chair for him. He sat.

Then I opened my copy of *D'Aulaires' Book of Greek Myths* and started reading.

ACKNOWLEDGMENTS

This book is very close to my heart. Once again, I owe deepest gratitude to my wonderful editor, Alyson Heller, and to Fiona Simpson and Mara Anastas of Aladdin/ Simon & Schuster for embracing this project so warmly. Jenna Stempel, a special thank-you for the beautiful cover art.

Jill Grinberg, you're the gold standard for agents as well as a dear friend. I can't possibly thank you enough for being in my corner. Katelyn Detweiler, Cheryl Pientka, and Denise St. Pierre, heartfelt thanks for all your expertise and support. I'm so proud to be on Team Jill.

I wish I didn't know my way around the Pediatrics floor of Memorial Sloan Kettering Cancer Center in New York, but that's where I met the many incredible people—patients, family members, doctors, and other health professionals—who contributed in various ways to this book. Deepest thanks to Dr. Julia Kearney, who first suggested a book about a normal

middle-school kid who survives cancer. Dr. Kearney gener-
ously shared her expertise and provided brilliant editorial
feedback on an early draft. My debt to her is endless. I'm also
so grateful for the help I received from other professionals at
MSKCC who have asked to remain anonymous.

I also wish to thank several former pediatric cancer
patients and their moms for candidly sharing their stories
with me: Helen Jonsen, Clare Watkins, Julia Brown, Jennifer
Brown, Eleanor Slate, Kelly Slate, Sloane Marcus, Robin Goetz
Chwatko. Scarlett Chwatko, in a few years you'll read this book
and let me know what I've gotten wrong. Helen, I wish we were
both members of a different club—but I'm so very grateful for
our friendship.

Violet Beller, thanks again for reading and providing terrific notes. Helen Perelman Bernstein, thanks for suggesting the
cover concept. Samantha Bernstein, thanks for sharing your
lovely Zentangle self-portrait.

When cancer strikes a kid, it's a thunderbolt aimed at
the whole family. Fortunately, our family is tough—especially
Alex, who read an early draft and provided incisive comments. Alex, your strength of character, insight, and empathy
will never cease to amaze me. I love and respect you like
crazy. Thank you for allowing me to tell this story—not your
story, of course, but of course your story was the inspiration.

As ever, I owe my daughter Lizzy bottomless gratitude for
several rounds of reading and editing (with her scary pencil),

as well as behind-the-scenes support. Josh, thanks for all your encouragement, counsel, and humor, which always keeps me going. Dani, an extra-special hug for all your bravery and goodness. And Chris: you're the best husband and father imaginable. You're also an amazing reader and editor, and I couldn't do this writing thing without you. Thanks for collaborating with me on absolutely everything. I love you.

**Don't miss another
great read from Barbara Dee!**

Boxes

WE GOT TO SCHOOL IN the dark that morning, already fifteen minutes late.

By then, cars were headed in the opposite direction, doggy heads hanging out the passenger windows, horns honking good-bye. Ms. Jordan was standing by the fancy bus, wearing jeans (*she owned jeans?*), checking her clipboard. She looked up; now I could see she was talking to Ava Seeley and her mom, a blond woman dressed head to toe in beige, like she was about to go on a safari.

Suddenly I had the feeling Ava was glaring at me. I mean,

my brain told me she wasn't; we were maybe thirty feet away from her, in a car, and probably she couldn't even see me through the windshield. But she was the head clonegirl of our grade, basically my enemy, so I was always on the lookout for her nasty expressions.

"Gug," I said, my stomach knotting.

"Tally, don't *decide* this will be bad before anything happens," Mom said.

"Yeah, well. Too late."

"Come on, honey, you got this." Mom gave me a pep smile, which usually worked. Although not this time. "Just share the goodies Dad baked you; that'll help with the bus trip. Oh, and here's a present from me."

She handed me a small sandwich bag. Inside were two red things that looked like cap erasers.

"Earplugs," Mom explained. "For the bus. And the room, if Ava's a snorer."

"If she is, she couldn't be louder than Spike." My dog was a champion loud breather, so I was an expert at ignoring snores. Obviously, Mom meant the earplugs for more than snoring.

I stuck the bag in my pants pocket and threw my arms around her. "Thanks, Mom."

She smooched my cheek. "You're welcome, Daughter. Text me when you get there, okay? Tell Spider to text his mom too. And let me help with the bakery boxes."

We stepped out of the car into the sharp, chilly air. It didn't even feel like September, really—although maybe that was because it still seemed liked night. Maybe once we were on the road, and the sun was up, it would feel like a normal fall morning in Eastview.

But not yet. I shivered.

Mom carried two of the boxes, and I carried one, plus my duffel bag. The bus had this huge underneath storage compartment, but by now it was completely crammed with everyone's stuff for the next four days. So we had to wedge my duffel in sideways, probably squishing all the extra cookies Dad had packed.

Then we walked over to Ms. Jordan.

"Good morning, Tally!" Ms. Jordan greeted me too energetically, as if she'd had an extra cup of coffee for breakfast. "I was starting to worry you wouldn't make it. You're Mrs. Martin?" she asked Mom.

Mom caught my eye. Because I'm so much bigger and taller than the rest of my family, people say stuff like this sometimes. Maybe Ms. Jordan didn't mean it as an actual question—*Are you really Tally's mom?*—but it was hard to tell.

"Yes, I am," Mom said, smiling at everyone. Even at Ava, who didn't bother to smile back.

But Ms. Jordan did. "Quite a daughter you have there. Full of character."

Mom nodded. You could tell she was trying to figure out whether that was a compliment.

Meanwhile, Ava's mom was reaching out her hand to shake Mom's, completely ignoring the fact that Mom was holding two bulging bakery boxes. "Good morning. I'm Ellen Seeley," she announced. "I'm the parent chaperone for this trip."

The parent chaperone? But there were three other parents going, I was sure of it.

"Oh yes," Mom said pleasantly. "We've already met, Ellen. How nice of you to volunteer! Tally, could I please give you these boxes? The car is in a no-parking zone, so I really can't stay." Her eyes were begging; she obviously wanted to escape Ellen Seeley.

"Sure," I said, stacking Mom's boxes on top of mine. "You'd better hurry, so you don't get a ticket."

Mom tiptoed to kiss my cheek. "Have fun, sweetheart,

and remember those earplugs," she murmured. "Tune out *whatever* you need to, okay? And don't forget to text." Then she raced off.

Mrs. Seeley turned to talk to Ms. Jordan, as Ava narrowed her eyes at me. "So what's in the boxes?" Ava asked.

"Oh, these?" I said. "Binoculars. Pickaxes. Flashlights. You know, assorted extremely high-tech devices for exploring our nation's capital."

"Huh," Ava said. She never appreciated my sense of humor. "It looks like bakery stuff."

"We're allowed to bring snacks," I informed her. "Not that I *am*."

"Whatever."

"What does *that* mean?"

"It means bring whatever you want, Tally. However *much* you want. I really don't care *what* you do, all right?"

"That's so funny, Ava," I replied. "Because you always act like exactly the opposite."

Now Ava definitely was glaring, and I glared right back at her. She was teeny, maybe ten inches shorter than me, so I had to stoop a bit to make eye contact. But it's hard to stoop while balancing three bakery boxes, so I sort of teetered in her direction.

Finally she said, "Well, you'd better get a seat. You're late, and we're about to leave."

And we know you'd hate to leave me behind, wouldn't you, Ava?

I climbed on board, my heart banging so loudly I was sure you could hear it over the bus engine.

Because here it was. We'd now arrived at the moment I'd been dreading for the past two weeks.

The moment I'd find out if my friends had shown up.

Or if I'd have to do this thing—all three days and four nights—stuck in a room alone with Ava Seeley.

We Hold These Truths

I STOOD AT THE FRONT of the crowded bus, balancing the boxes, scanning the rows. Where were they? Had Sonnet and Spider chickened out, the way I was terrified they would? Especially Spider, who'd texted me at eleven last night: Umm, not so sure about this. . . .

Nono, it will be fun!!!! I'd texted back.

But he'd never answered, which meant I hadn't slept very much, even with Spike's cuddling.

I looked past all the clonegirls in the front rows, then Mr. Gianelli and the chaperones: Mia Gilroy's mom, Althea

Packer's mom, Jamal Melton's dad. Finally I spotted Sonnet waving at me from the second-to-last row.

I breathed.

Then, clutching the boxes with sweaty hands, I made my way down the aisle, past classmates who were either half-asleep or much too perky for five fifteen in the morning.

The way this sort of fancy bus worked was: window, two seats together, aisle, one seat, window. I guess to save the entire row, Sonnet and Spider had split up, with Sonnet sitting by the window in the two-seat part, and Spider across the aisle by himself. So, like usual, my seat was in the middle—next to Sonnet, across the aisle from Spider.

But also right in front of Marco Sarris and Trey Donaldson. Which meant that for the next six and one-quarter hours, there'd be no vacation from Spider's possibly-former-but-I-wasn't-sure-about-this enemies.

Oh, bleep.

"Where *were* you, Tally?" Spider was asking. "Why were you late?" His soft brown eyes were enormous.

"Sorry," I said, handing him the top box. "Dad insisted on making cinnamon buns this morning. And then of course he had to do the icing. You didn't think I'd just forget to *show*, did you?"

I recycled Mom's pep smile for him, but he didn't smile back.

"Nah, I knew you'd make it," Spider admitted. He opened the box. "Whoa, awesome. Your dad rules."

"He definitely does," I said, giving the second box to Sonnet. "These are from the bakery. He made them yesterday, but they're still pretty fresh."

She squealed when she saw the box had giant chocolate chip cookies. My box had some Cinna-mmm muffins and a few blondies. To be honest, the cookies and blondies kind of made me queasy this hour of the morning, but I figured I'd change my mind about them later.

"We can trade," I announced as I settled into my seat. "Plus there's a ton more stuff in my duffel bag. Dad kind of went crazy with the bakery products. I barely had room for my treasure box."

"Wait," Sonnet said. "You brought your treasure box, Tally?" She asked this quietly, like it was a secret between the two of us.

"Yeah, of course. I'd never travel without my treasures. Why would I?"

"I don't know. Ms. Jordan said not to bring precious things on the trip, right?"

"Well, but they're not 'precious things.' Just precious to *me*."

"But what if they get lost or something?"

"That's why I brought the treasure box. So they *won't* get lost."

"I know, but." Sonnet began chewing on her thumbnail. "Maybe they're too precious for this trip."

Sonnet always dressed in such a careful, boring way— all her tops the colors of fall fruit, little gold studs in her ears, nothing in her straight black hair but a red ponytail holder—so probably she didn't understand why I needed my treasures with me. But I knew she thought they were cool, because she said so all the time. She even used that specific word: "cool."

Was Sonnet worried that they wouldn't be safe in a room with Ava? Or was she worried about something else? Either way, it was extremely strange.

I glanced over at Spider. He was fine, just eating a bun and reading one of his space books. I didn't envy a whole lot about him, but the way he could read wherever—in moving vehicles, the noisy cafeteria, dark movie theaters—seemed kind of like a superpower, really. And he didn't even need earplugs.

A jab on my shoulder.

"Hey, Math Girl, your dad *baked* you all of that?" Marco was practically hanging over my seat, salivating like a cartoon wolf.

"Yeah," I said. "He's a baker. So you know, he bakes."

"Cool. You're so lucky."

"Yeah, I know."

"Wish someone in *my* family baked like that."

Obviously, he was waiting for me to offer him something. Well, too bad for him. I didn't forget things so easily. And I didn't feel the need to bribe him. At least, not yet.

Sonnet's cheeks were already bulging with cookie. "Eelikeshoo," she murmured.

"What?" I said.

She chewed and swallowed. Then she leaned over and whispered with chocolate breath: "He likes you."

"Don't be preposterous."

"No, no, I mean it. He asked if you'd be sitting here when he took the seat."

"Well, that was stupid. Of *course* I'd be, if you and Spider were here."

Suddenly Sonnet did a bizarre thing: *She passed her box of cookies to Trey and Marco.* "You should try these; they're amazing," she told them, blushing.

I kicked her in the shin.

She looked at me blankly, so I pulled out my phone and texted her:

Me: Why did you do that?

Her: Why not?

Me: Dad baked for ME to share with MY FRIENDS. They are NOT MY FRIENDS!!!

Her: Well maybe they could be, if we're nice they could be nice back

Me: ARE YOU SERIOUS

Her: yeah Why not

Me: !!!!they bullied Spider!!!!

Her: Well people change, I dunno they seem nice now

I couldn't believe this. The cookies weren't even Sonnet's; I'd just handed them to her for the trip. So what right did she have to pass them to an Evil Nemesis—or to anyone, really?

Finally Ms. Jordan, Ava's mom, and Ava climbed onto the bus. Ms. Jordan said something to the driver, Ava took her seat with Nadia Ramirez and the other clonegirls they hung out with, and *brrmm*, we were off.

We'd barely pulled out of Eastview before these girls

started singing *Hamilton*. Haley Spriggs, of course, was the loudest; she had the best voice, too, so she was Angelica, Ava was Eliza, and Nadia Ramirez was Peggy:

> *We hold these truths to be self-evident*
> *That all men are created equal*

And Sonnet was singing right along with them. Of course, they couldn't hear her all the way in the back of the bus, but the funny thing was how her singing was a decibel too loud, like she was hoping that somehow her voice would carry to their seats, and they'd come racing down the aisle with their arms outstretched: *Ooh, look, our long-lost Schuyler sister!*

A weird question popped into my head: *Does Sonnet wish she was sitting in the front, with the clonegirls, singing along? Maybe she does. And considering how she's rooming with that awful Haley Spriggs—*

Okay, click on a different thought, I ordered myself.

I peeked at Spider, who turned a page in his book. He'd tuned everything out, it seemed. Including me.

And suddenly Ava's voice—high and piercing, surprisingly

strong for such a teeny person—took over the bus, drowning out everything, including the bus engine.

> *Look around, look around,*
> *At how lucky we are to be alive right now—*

I stuck in the earplugs and shut my eyes.

ABOUT THE AUTHOR

BARBARA DEE is the author of nine middle-grade novels published by Simon & Schuster, including *Everything I Know About You*, *Halfway Normal*, and *Star-Crossed*. Her books have received several starred reviews and been included on many best-of lists, including the ALA Rainbow List Top Ten, the Chicago Public Library Best of the Best, and the NCSS-CBC Notable Social Studies Trade Books for Young People. *Star-Crossed* was also a Goodreads Choice Awards finalist. Barbara is one of the founders of the Chappaqua Children's Book Festival. She lives with her family, including a naughty cat named Luna and a sweet rescue hound dog named Ripley, in Westchester County, New York.

Looking for another great book?
Find it
IN THE MIDDLE.

Fun, fantastic books for kids
in the in-be**TWEEN** age.

IntheMiddleBooks.com

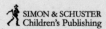